Claim

The Sigma Menace: Book 1

By Marie Johnston

Fever Claim

Copyright © 2014 by Lisa Elijah

Copyediting by EbookEditingServices.com

2nd Edition Editing: The Killion Group

Cover by P and N Graphics

After being ditched only weeks before her wedding, Cassie Stockwell wasn't out looking for a hookup. Then the devastatingly handsome bartender she'd been trying not to obsess over for months offered to give her a ride home. What could one night hurt?

When his future was almost taken away after one impulsive decision, wolf-shifter Jace Miller waited patiently for months before making a move on the woman he knew to be his destined mate. But will one night of passion keep his little human by his side once she learns of his world and the danger it brings to her doorstep?

For all the latest news, excerpts, and deleted scenes, sign up for my newsletter at www.mariejohnstonwriter.com.

To my own mate, Kris. Thanks for having my back.

Chapter One

"Hey, hot bartender!" Cassie lifted her empty shot glass. "Absolutely Screwed over here."

If she wasn't on her third shot, she was pretty sure she wouldn't be calling the bartender anything. Or leaning over the bar to bare a little extra cleavage, a category she wasn't doing so bad in. But the name of the mandarin vodka orange juice drink and getting dumped on her ass by her fiancé two weeks before the wedding, well, they just seemed to go together, and tonight she wasn't going to analyze it.

Hot Bartender flicked his intense gaze to hers, and gave a slight nod. Cassie slid off the surface of the bar and plopped back onto her bar stool with a sigh.

What'd you expect? She examined her empty glass, dejected by his lack of interest. She came into Pale Moonlight pretty frequently. It was her bestie Kaitlyn's favorite hangout. In all the times she'd been in here the last ten months, she scarcely had the courage to even look at Hot Bartender. Of course, several of those times had been with her fiancé, oops—ex-fiancé, Grant, so it's not like she'd been looking for male attention. Hot Bartender was in a different category of male and she was positive his *attention* would also be a different category. But his brand of male attention was not on her. He barely acknowledged her each time he set her drink down in front of her.

Cassie knew she wasn't his type, or anyone else's in this establishment, with its high ratio of tall, brawny males and underdressed females. Pale Moonlight had a reputation for being austere, and not just in aesthetics. The shockingly gorgeous men and women who owned and worked the club were notorious for not tolerating fights, unwanted groping (because it was obvious there was a lot of *wanted* groping), or illicit dealings of the illegal variety. Regardless, the club had a lot of loyalty with the local crowd.

The majority of that loyalty had to do with the back rooms dubbed The Den. Cassie had heard bits of gossip of what went on in those rooms. Hell, she'd seen enough to support the whispers—heavily muscled men leading scantily clad, eager women off the dance floor, disappearing into the hallway leading to the rooms that made up The Den. She'd watched with interest as those same men led the women back out, supporting them on their now weak, unsteady legs. Cassie dubbed them Jelly Girls because of their rubbery legs. The women always appeared to be in a state of post-coital bliss, with rumpled outfits and bedroom hair. They were passed on to the employees, who took the charges from there, leading them back to their group or out of the club. She'd watched astonished as the men would then beckon another interested, under-dressed, attractive woman and disappear with her back down the hallway.

Being a psychologist for living, she sometimes forgot she wasn't beyond being shocked. *To each their own.* They all seemed to be consenting enough. Cassie gave a mental snort. *At least someone was going to consent tonight, probably over and over again, too.*

"What's with the hard liquor tonight, Tinkerbell?" a smooth, deep voice asked her.

With a start, Cassie's gaze flew up and realized the panty-melting voice came from Hot Bartender. A new drink was in front of her, and so was he, leaning on both arms on the bar.

Alcohol fueling her courage and taking advantage of his proximity, she let her eyes roam over him. When she first came in here all those months ago and saw him behind the bar, she was too pussy to even look directly at him since her first impression was of the sheer masculinity he possessed. He was probably close to six and a half feet tall; imposing enough compared to her five and a half feet. She knew his eyes were the palest blue, like ice, and his head was shaved, but this close she could see the dark stubble covering his scalp and chiseled jaw. Thick, short, dark lashes rimmed his eyes and he possessed equally dark arching eyebrows.

She was following the intricate artwork tatted into the muscles on the side of his neck and running down into his tight-fitting shirt. *Mmmm... bet his body is a work of art judging from the fit of his shirt. He must be nothing but muscles and ink and more muscles. How far does that ink travel down? Are those scars under the tattoos? That's hot.*

"Tinkerbell?" he repeated. Cassie's gaze flew back up to his face. He cocked an eyebrow and there was a hint of amusement in his eyes. A flush of embarrassment worked up her neck to her face. Oh hell. She took and swallowed the shot.

"Uh, what?" The Absolutely Screwed drink was more accurate than ever. Hot Bartender just busted her ogling and that was another thing Pale Moonlight didn't tolerate, making any advances on their staff. It happened (duh! look at them), but when the woman was leggy, with fuck-me hair and stripper heels in a painted-on dress, well they got away with more. Cassie was medium height, too curvy to wear anything formfitting—well, she could (and she'd rock it, thank you very much) but men's hooker radars started to malfunction and she would have to slap someone. So she usually just wore her clothes from work; they were as sedate and boring as she was. Adding to that image was her non-highlighted, uncolored plain brown hair in a low maintenance pixie cut. Speaking of which—

"Did you just call me Tinkerbell?"

The other eyebrow rose up to meet the first cocked brow. "Yeah, it fits you."

"Does it?" she uttered, a little dumbstruck. Hot Bartender was flirting with her. Hopes... almost up... nah, it was his job. She shrugged. "Well, I guess there's worse things to be called. Can I get another Absolutely Screwed, please?"

"One more coming right up. But that's all, Tink. When they hit you, it'll be fast and hard."

"Well, that's how I like it, Hot Bartender," Cassie said, a bit irritated. Did he cut everyone off after three—*four?*—shots? She was a grown ass woman. One who just got left at the altar, no less. Keep. Them. Coming.

"Do you, now?" Hot Bartender's eyed flared with heat that was gone by the time her mind registered the innuendo she'd just put out there. Then he moved down the bar to mix her drink.

Ugh! How many bad come-on lines must he hear? Now the name Cassandra Stockwell can be added to his Desperate Lonely Women That Hit On Me At Work list.

I'm not desperate, dammit! Cassie reassured herself. *Just really pissed.* Trying to be discrete, she watched him work, his actions quick and confident, his muscles rippling through his black shirt. She'd been in once, maybe twice, a month since Kaitlyn found the place, but was always too afraid she'd be kicked out for staring at him like she was researching her new book *How to Stalk the Hot Bartender*. And she might still be thrown out if she didn't stop gawking. She tore her gaze away from him to the dance floor to look for Kaitlyn.

The hard rock music blaring through the club wasn't really her thing, but the beat had her tapping her foot. That's the closest she got to dancing. Kaitlyn, on the other hand, was out there with a guy Cassie had never seen in here before. Kaitlyn's tall, willowy body slid up and down Mystery Man, somehow simultaneously riding his knee. Mystery Man had undone Kaitlyn's long coppery locks. Her hair swung on her back while he rested his hands low on her slender hips and murmured into her ear. Maybe Cassie didn't know what he was saying, but could assume his words were meant to entice Kaitlyn's clothes off at the end of the night. Aaaaand they'd probably work.

"You didn't answer my question. What's with the hard stuff?" Hot Bartender was back. And still trying to talk to her?

She swiveled back on her stool to face him. Dammit, the room spun on her. "Well, if you must know. I was getting married in two weeks and I got dumped two hours ago. So, here I am—absolutely screwed and drinking my new favorite shot." Cassie downed the rest of her shot.

He was in front of her like before, propped against the counter, watching her throat work as the citrusy liquid burned its way down. The heat returned to his eyes as he followed her hand that wiped away the remnants of the drink. It was a busy night in the club, but he was hanging out in front of her like he had all the time in the world. The other guy behind the bar, also extremely good looking, sporting the same uber bad boy image as Hot Bartender, was fielding all the drink orders, taking it in stride that he was left to handle the crowd on his own. But it was not like anyone was going to complain about the service to these two tall, almost sinister-looking men.

He nodded once, his pale gaze still resting on her. Her heart thumped a little harder and it wasn't from the vodka. The rest of her body warmed, centering on her core.

"He wasn't right for you," he said simply.

"What?" Incredulous, Cassie half shouted her question, taken by surprise. "Why would you think that?"

He leaned over the bar a little farther. "Tinkerbell, you've been coming in with him for months and not once did I see him light you up."

"Light me up?" She shook her head, marveling over this conversation with this man. This man who made her heart race just looking at him, made her insides turn molten when he looked at her, made her squirm in her seat hearing his voice.

"You two didn't dance. You didn't sit on each other's lap. You seldom held hands." He nodded his head toward the dance floor. "Your friend out there has had more action during this song than I've ever seen between you and your ex."

Cassie's mouth dropped open. Normally, she'd take a breath and analyze the situation before she said anything. She'd paid a lot of money for a lot of years of school to be able to do that. Mandarin vodka fueled her angry words. "What do you know about any of it? We loved each other, we respected each other. All you see here," she gestured around her, "is lust. Nothing more."

Hot Bartender leaned in even closer to her. "So you didn't lust for him?" His low voice vibrated through her, making her shiver. *Dear Lord.* With him this close, she caught his scent—all male and like he hung his fresh linen in the woods. Her already warmed core throbbed to the beat of its own music and her breasts grew full and heavy.

"Tell me, Tink," he continued, "have you been sitting here mourning your lost love? Or have you been running through all the logistics of canceling the wedding and tallying exactly how much you'll be out once all is said and done?"

He had a lot of balls to ask her that. She was heartbroken, dammit! Grant was a nice man; they loved each other. Well, she thought they did until he stopped at her place earlier asking for his ring back because "this all just felt wrong" and he "needed to find himself." She didn't even want to think about the logistics of canceling everything, other than she was only bothering with trying to get money back from anything she'd sunk any of her own money into. Her mental list of calls to make on Monday was growing: there was the florist, the travel agent, the—damn that wall of man in front of her!

"There are five stages of grief. I'm working on anger right now." Cassie took a calming breath. Her thinking was getting fuzzy as she wasn't used to surpassing her limit of one glass of wine. Sometimes, she'd even have two, if it'd been a particularly shitty day at work dealing with her pretentious coworker, Dr. Ego, or patients careening over the deep end. On those occasions, she was at home in her flannel pajama pants and tank top. "I'd like another drink please, Hot Bartender."

Still leaning on the bar, he pointed to a glass of clear liquid with ice already set beside her. "Have some water."

"Wha—," she sputtered, "I've only had, like, three drinks."

"Four. In an hour. You need some water." He slid the water in front of her. "Drink."

"Uh, Hot Bartender, I plan to drink 'til I forget tonight. And water won't make that happen. I even have a driver lined up." Despite her bravado, she picked up the water and sucked on the straw.

His eyes darkened as they followed the straw and watched her lips wrap around it. "One, my name is Jace. Two, your driver might be sober, but is probably going home with someone else tonight."

"Jace." She tested his name out and watched as a look of pure male satisfaction settled on his face. "Nice to meet you, Jace. I'm Cassie." She took another sip from the straw.

"My pleasure, Cassie," he murmured, watching her lips again. Entranced by his reaction to her drinking, she watched him watching her.

"O-M-G, Cassie!" Kaitlyn bounded up next to her. "You'll never believe what happened." She rushed on. "I met Tyson on the dance floor. He has a Roadster and offered to take me for a ride."

Cassie rolled her eyes. Typical, impulsive Kaitlyn. She flitted from adventure to adventure, to the men who were involved in each circumstance, and moved on just as quickly.

"And you'll be back when?" Cassie asked. Getting drunk at the bar with a friend after getting dumped didn't smack of pathetic loneliness like getting drunk at the bar alone after getting dumped.

Kaitlyn giggled. "It'll be a quick ride. Do I ever leave you hanging?"

Cassie raised an eyebrow. She'd been left hanging enough to have learned to either drive herself or bring Grant for conversation, as she was usually left at the table while Kaitlyn attached herself to the first willing dance partner and often left with him. Why would tonight be any different?

"Go ahead. I'll call a cab." Ugh, she hated that idea. What else was there? Be the third wheel while Tyson gave her a lift? Or worse, he'd be like "Hey, you two are friends… have you ever kissed?" Wouldn't be the first time one of Kaitlyn's dates had that great idea.

"I'll make sure you get home okay," Jace said.

Surprised, Kaitlyn finally noticed he was still standing there. "Oh," she breathed, eyeing Jace, "I'm sure you will." She turned to Cassie with a huge smile, her eyes twinkling mischievously.

"I'll be fine," Cassie said quickly, suddenly embarrassed to be getting ditched in front of Jace by her friend after her answer to his "why the hard liquor" question. Now he was taking her on as a charity case. "Go, have fun."

Kaitlyn leaned in to Cassie and gave her a big hug. "You're a rock star. Drink 'til you forget and he'll call you a cab, 'kay?"

As Kaitlyn turned to go, Cassie grabbed her arm. "You be safe, all right?"

"Of course." Kaitlyn laughed as she bounced off toward Tyson who was leaning against the exit. He was Kaitlyn's type: tall, good-looking, dressed casually in jeans and a sweater that probably cost more than at least half of Cassie's wardrobe.

Wishing she could still ride high on the nice buzz she had going, Cassie did her best to avoid Jace's gaze and dug out her phone. She was throwing in the towel and calling a cab.

"Put that away, Cassie. I'll take you home," Jace spoke quietly, but she heard him clearly over the music. Her fingers hesitated punching in the search option for taxis. "We can drive your car so you have it in the morning and won't need to make plans to come back and get it."

Cassie looked up at him, into his pale-blue eyes. He looked calmly at her, but he barely seemed to be breathing, as if everything hinged on her agreement. What could a man like him want with a girl like her? They were from different worlds. Maybe it was just to drive her home, out of the goodness of his heart. Make sure she got into her condo safely, then walk to the nearest bus stop and head back. He couldn't be *interested* interested, could he?

Testing the waters she said, "Then how will you get back?"

"You wanted to forget, Cassie." Jace seductively gave her a once over from the other side of the bar. "I'll help you forget. Again and again. Let me take you home."

Ooookaaaay. Well, that answered her question. The shaved-headed, dangerous-looking bartender wanted to walk on the wild side of her silk blouse, neutral colored slacks, kitten-heeled wearing self. She would ride high on that buzz she had going on. And by riding high, she meant on Jace.

She passed him her keys. "I'll meet you by the Honda Civic out front."

***

"OHMYGOD! OHMYGOD!" Cassie screamed as Jace pounded into her from behind. "Yes! Yes!" He had her on her hands and knees, completely naked and he was on his knees behind her, pants undone but otherwise fully clothed.

Jace couldn't believe he finally had her right where he wanted her. Needed her. He would make her his after the close call of almost losing her. He'd been watching her come into his club for months. He knew exactly who she was when he first saw her walk in, wearing her standard professional wear as if she had just come from the office. She was average height, with short hair that probably started the day with no-nonsense styling but ended up falling into a sassy do by the time she came into the club. She hardly wore makeup. She didn't need to, having a clean, fresh appeal he didn't see often working at the club. Both her hair and her eyes were chestnut brown, reflecting natural highlights from her surroundings, not needing cosmetic enhancements. She was a natural beauty and she exuded intelligence in everything she did.

Mine, he'd thought then as he watched her, and that same friend she was with tonight, walk to an open table. The utter dismay he'd felt when he saw a man walk in after them, help her take her coat off, and sit next to her with his arm draped over the back of her chair, almost brought out his beast.

He was a patient male and didn't want to scare her off. Knowing his looks and the first impression they gave women, that he wanted to fuck them or kill them—or both—Jace decided to bide his time. Wait for her and Mr. Wrong to break things off. It would never work between those two, she'd have to feel how wrong it was eventually. She'd have to.

But she didn't. Jace remained patient, watching her discreetly each time she came in. He knew her scent by now, and even across the crowded club, she hadn't smelled like Mr. Wrong. She smelled like she'd been around him, but not intimate. And that was the only thing keeping Mr. Wrong alive. Jace had to make sure he didn't react first and think later, but knew that if he caught the musk of sex on her and it wasn't from him, his beast would win. He had paid too much already, lost too much. He wouldn't lose her, too. He had put his special *ability* to good use and influence her boyfriend… just a little. Whenever the guy came up to the bar for a drink, Jace looked him in the eyes and gave him a mental nudge to keep his dick away from Cassie.

She never acknowledged Jace, never spoke to him. Fuck, she barely even looked at him. He seethed when he'd watch those two leave together and try not to imagine what rights Mr. Dead Meat might be granted to her body if his influence didn't hold.

Then her friend, Kaitlyn, had contacted the club manager about a bridal shower. Jace explained his situation to Christian, Pale Moonlight's owner, and got the wedding date. With only weeks to spare, it was time Jace paid Mr. Soon-to-be-Ex a personal visit.

When Cassie walked into the club tonight, Jace resolved he would not risk another close call. He would do everything he could to make her his. Her drinks had a more mandarin juice than vodka; he wouldn't let her get drunk. He needed her acceptance, wanted her reactions to him to be real and not leave her feeling sick and empty the next day.

Earlier, when she slid the keys across to him, his heart had soared. He'd controlled his reaction as he nodded to Christian, walked out, and opened the car door for Cassie. As soon as he folded himself into her sedan, he inhaled the scent that was uniquely her without the chaotic smells that flowed through the club. Her scent matched her natural beauty, a floral scent that made him think of running through green pastures dotted with wildflowers in full bloom. He immediately hardened, straining against his zipper, tempted to lean the seats back and take her right there in front of the club. But for what he had in mind, they needed to be where they could have space and plenty of interruption-free hours.

Cassie had given him directions to her place as he raced through streets, doing the minimum to not get pulled over or have an accident. When they arrived, he parked in her garage and closed them both in. He hesitated. Was she ready for this, not going to change her mind? If he had to wait longer for her, he would. It'd fucking kill him, but he'd wait.

She entered her condo and looked up through her lashes, almost shyly, at him and he leaned down to capture her mouth. Sweet Mother Earth, he had never imagined her taste. She was sweet from her fruity drinks and her mouth fit his perfectly. He groaned, his shaft hardening further, wanting release from his jeans. Not yet. Jace picked her up and she wrapped her legs around him, and he stepped across the threshold and kicked the door shut, then reached behind and locked it.

Jace coaxed her mouth open and used his tongue to mimic what he had planned for her lush body later. Cassie looped her arms around his neck and pulled his head closer. The little coos she made were almost his undoing. His hands roamed up her torso, loving the feel of her curves, and pulled her shirt up, caressing her soft skin underneath up to cup her breasts. They filled his big hands as if they were made for him.

Breaking contact to lift her blouse up over her head, he had gone back to sampling her sweet, wet mouth. She tugged up his shirt, wanting to do her own exploring. He knelt down there in the foyer, and, still holding her, unclasped her bra straps with one hand while cupping her bottom with his other.

Her breasts had bounced free and he groaned again, groping one, rubbing his thumb to tease her nipple. He'd love to give them the attention they deserved, but they would have to wait. Carefully, he laid her down, coming down on top of her, supporting his weight on his knees and forearms so he could finish undressing her while he still had her mouth captured with his.

Cassie hands skimmed up and down his back, around and up and down his front. She was getting bolder, roaming closer to his zipper where his arousal strained to reach her. Just one touch and he'd be lost.

He undid her pants and, still kissing her, peeled them down. Once he tossed them aside, he slid his hand between her thighs and found her wet and ready. She bowed into him as he slid a finger between her folds and swirled in slow circles.

"Oh, Jace," she gasped, as she arched in his hand again. Male pride swelled in him; there was no mistaking who made her feel like this. He inserted a finger inside of her. Her legs fell farther open and she matched his rhythm. He inserted another finger into her channel as he continued massaging her slick heat.

The pressure built, both of them gasped for more. He pulled his hand away. "Flip over," he commanded, as he used his other hand to unzip his pants.

Desperate for her release, Cassie had immediately rolled over onto hands and knees, lifting her bottom into the air, stretching back to him. Jace looked his fill as he palmed himself and got into position behind her. Her curves were astounding—a firm rounded ass that tapered for her slender waist and flared back out at the bust to give her a perfect hourglass figure. Smooth, creamy skin softer than he could have ever imagined a woman could have slid under his hands as he held her in place.

She looked at him over her shoulder, her dark eyes pleading with him to finish what he started. The complete ecstasy as he slowly entered her stole his breath. She was tight but wet. He gritted his teeth to keep himself from surging forward and hurting her. Her body was greedy for his length as he fed himself in inch by inch. Finally, he was settled in completely and he paused to let her body get used to his size. His kind was usually well-endowed and he was no exception.

She made a mewling sound and stretched back against him. He slid out, and back in. They had groaned in unison. Perfection. It was then Jace allowed himself to thrust freely. He pounded a rhythm that would drive them both to heights only mates could experience together. This was what he waited months for and if he wasn't mistaken, what she'd also waited months for.

Cassie cried out and clenched further around him. Jace's balls tightened and rose, he leaned over her bracing one hand on the floor, the other arm around Cassie's middle, holding her close while he thrust behind her. When her orgasm overtook her and she bucked wildly underneath him, screaming, his own seed rose with his impending orgasm. At last he could lay claim to his destined mate. Jace opened his mouth wide and bit hard where her neck met her shoulder, sharp teeth sinking into her flushed skin.

Cassie's cries strengthened as her orgasm grew more powerful, both with the bite and Jace's seed flowing into her, marking her as his forever.

Breathing heavily, Jace's body shook as his orgasm faded, almost taking the use of his legs from him. He gently helped Cassie stretch out on the floor beneath him. Still inside her, he licked where he had bitten her, and felt her shiver and sigh. He trailed tiny kisses across her shoulder as he slipped out of her and rolled her over.

Her eyes were half-lidded, with a dreamy smile on her face. By the Sweet Mother, she was glorious. He kissed her hard and deeply. She returned his kiss, gliding her hands back up under his shirt. He pulled away and pulled his shirt over his head, and tossed it, loving the greedy way she was looking at him.

Now he'd take his time, explore her with his hands and mouth. He looked at her body. Her large breasts were topped with rosy nipples that beaded under his perusal. He leaned his head down and swirled his tongue around the tip as he massaged her other breast. He settled between her legs and heard her gasp.

"Again?" she breathed.

Jace chuckled, "Tinkerbell, I'm not even close to done with you yet."

Chapter Two

C assie slept in late. From the sunlight streaming through her bedroom window, it must be late. She didn't know what time they'd made it to bed, once they did make it to the actual bed. But Jace hadn't been done with her then, either. She'd finally passed out in utter exhaustion in the early morning hours, wrapped in his embrace.

She sat up on the edge of bed and noted with dismay the other side was empty. Not wanting to dwell much on what happened last night yet, let alone the empty bed, she sat up and groaned, rubbing her eyes. She had a major cotton mouth she could contribute to the combo of shots and hours of screaming orgasms. A full glass of water rested on her nightstand. Cassie wondered what to make of the considerate gesture. He jetted before she woke up, but stayed long enough to leave her water? Gulping it down, she got up and stumbled to the master bath. On the way there, she snatched her favorite flannel bottoms and a tank top.

The floor of the bathroom was still wet. Jace must've showered not long ago. At least he didn't leave immediately, or hadn't been worried she'd sleep through it. Between that and the glass of water waiting for her, she felt a little better about what she'd done last night with an almost complete stranger—a mind-numbingly hot, insatiable stranger, with a ridiculous body. Cassie turned on the shower and hopped in, memories of last night running through her mind.

After Jace—would she ever be able to think of him without developing a full-body blush?—had his way with her in the foyer, he'd lifted her boneless body and carried her to the bedroom. He placed her on the bed and stood back to watch her through heavy-lidded eyes, and hardened again.

The moonlight streaming through her blinds had showcased his body—muscle rippled from head to toes, eight-pack washboard stomach with firm buttocks and solid legs. He was a work of art, a bronze statue of male perfection.

She had patted the bed next to her, desperate for her turn to pleasure him. His eyes darkened as he climbed next to her and stretched out. Cassie took her time roaming his chest with her hands and mouth. Jace groaned, now fully erect, and rolled onto his back giving her free reign over him. She eased further down, wrapping her hand around his fullness. He pivoted his hips up into her hand as she slowly stroked him.

Getting up onto her knees, still holding onto him, she guided him into her mouth.

"Cassie," Jace breathed. She loved hearing him say her name, loved that she could drive him wild.

She swirled her tongue over the crown and pumped her fist at the base, using her other hand to massage his heavy sac. Jace gripped the back of her head as she matched her mouth and hands in a synchronous rhythm. Soon he urged her to straddle him.

Cassie took her time sliding down Jace's length, with his hands guiding her backside. He watched her intently as she rode him. Her breaths came faster and faster as another orgasm quickly built. She leaned into him, arms around his broad shoulders, nuzzling his neck. Jace reached between them to rub her sensitive spot, while his other hand lightly held her head to his throat.

The orgasm slammed into her. When she opened her mouth wide to cry out, she instead bit his neck. He tensed as his orgasm hit him and he roared, bucking wildly beneath her.

Oh my God, I bit him. Cassie shut off the shower with a groan. It'd felt so instinctual and natural at the time, but it was so unlike her. She didn't do random and wild like she had last night. Good thing he was gone or she'd have to look him in the eye and act normal instead of searching him for her bite marks. *Bite marks!* She turned to look at her back in the mirror finding his teeth marks from when he first took her.

Her fingers trailed over the red marks fading at the base of her neck. She traced the impressions of two longer teeth, his canines. Tiny zings of electricity flowed through her each time she put pressure on the marks. The sensations were infinitesimal compared to the initial bite when her release was imminent, built up stronger than she ever thought possible. His mouth had closed on his mark and it was like lightening shot from her neck, to her center, to where he thrust inside of her.

She gave a quick shake of her head in hopes it would cease the slow throb that started between her legs as soon as thoughts of biting ran through her mind. She combed her short hair, and climbed into her pajamas. When she opened the bathroom door, she stopped short. *What was that smell? Bacon?*

Cassie rushed from her bedroom to the kitchen. Surprised, she took in the scene before her. There was Jace, with his back to her, standing at her stove scrambling eggs. He wore his jeans from last night but that was all. The muscles in his broad back rippled, his biceps flexing each time he scraped the spatula. Jace, standing at her stove with bare feet lent more to any intimacy between them than anything they'd done in the last twelve hours. She should be spooked. Instead her heart fluttered at the possessiveness and domesticity of him cooking for her.

Jace flicked the stove off and glanced at her over his shoulder. His pale blue eyes soaked her in, his hungry gaze hinted that if didn't have a hot pan full of food in his hands, they'd be repeating one or two of their previous performances. She nervously shifted her weight.

"You okay?" he asked.

"Um… yeah… I'd thought you'd left." She hadn't realized how much it would have bothered her had he been truly gone.

"Nope. I thought we could have a bite to eat. How you feeling?"

On cue, her stomach rumbled. She pushed her bangs off her face. "Yeah," she said slowly, "no, I'm good. Good. Thanks for the water." *Stellar conversation, Dr. Stockwell.*

He nodded toward the table with two glasses of orange juice and two plates, each with a pile of bacon. "Have a seat. The eggs are done so we can eat."

Apparently, he was better at this morning-after stuff than she was. She walked stiffly to her little table and sat a bit gingerly. She wasn't as stiff and sore as she thought she should be. It's not like she had a sex life like that with Grant.

Ah, fuck—Grant! The memories of why she was in this situation flooded back. Well, there went reconciliation. She wouldn't want to enter a marriage after a day's break in the relationship that included a long, passionate night with another person. Long and passionate weren't words she'd use to describe her love life with Grant. They'd been… compatible. At least in the beginning. Lately, even make-out sessions were few and far between. He just hadn't seemed interested. She used the excuse they were saving up for after the wedding. To make it more exciting, right?

Cassie took a deep breath to slow her thinking and organize her thoughts. Her engagement was good and over. She'd figure out Grant's reasons later. It was only Saturday; she'd worry about canceling wedding plans and notifying guests come Monday. Now all she needed to figure out was this bartender, who normally oozed malice and danger with his disconcerting eyes and shaved head, but thoughtfully left her water and cooked her breakfast.

He emptied the pan onto their plates and set it on the counter, then took a seat across from her. He quietly watched her, gauging her reaction. "Go ahead and eat Cassie." Her name on his lips warmed her, the sensation moving through to her core… impossible that after last night she could be ready to go again so easily.

Jace inhaled sharply, his gaze darkened and he readjusted himself under the table. "Let's eat, first. Then we'll…" he eyed her breasts, her nipples hard under her top, "talk."

She nodded dumbly and picked up a bacon slice. After the first bite, she inhaled the food, completely famished. She was swallowing the rest of her orange juice when she looked back up at him. His plate was also empty, his hands folded in front of him, quietly watching her, amused.

Searching for something to do that wouldn't betray how nervous and awkward she felt, she picked up her glass and plate, and collected his dishes, too. His eyes trailed over her body and she swore she could feel the heat of the path they took.

What was it she said at the bar last night? *It's lust, nothing more.* This felt like more. He'd always made her aware she was a woman with a healthy sex drive. She was conscious to never stare at him at the bar, telling herself she didn't want to get on management's bad side. She also felt it was rude to Grant to ogle other men, especially if he was with her. Grant never cared for Pale Moonlight, he only went with her knowing how much Kaitlyn meant to Cassie. And since Cassie hardly went out otherwise, he was happy to oblige. Reminiscing about Grant's kindness sent a pang of remorse through her. She'd analyze those thoughts later, too.

Cassie set the dishes in the sink. *Think Dr. Stockwell. Analyze the situation. What are the important points you're missing?* It helped her straighten her thoughts out when she referred to herself by her professional title. It reminded her of all the blood, sweat, and tears she put into her education, and that she was more than equipped to figure out any situation she found herself in. She just never expected to find herself in a situation like this.

"So," she began, "thanks for breakfast."

He shrugged. "No problem." He was reclining back in his chair, arms crossed over his big chest, his long legs kicked out and crossed in front of him.

She leaned her hip against the counter, trying to figure out what else to say. He mentioned wanting to talk and she couldn't imagine about what. She wanted to start with why he was still there. But the thought of him leaving made her gut clench. She liked seeing him in her place, wished she hadn't missed him rummaging through her cabinets. Bizarre.

She always knew what to say and her brain wasn't fuzzy, considering last night's alcohol and the mountain of pure male relaxing at her kitchen table, her thoughts should be unclear. Yet her thinking was just fine…

"I don't know where to begin—" Jace started.

"Did you do something to my drink?" Cassie blurted.

A hint of amusement lit his face as he considered his answer. "Yes. I gave you more juice, less vodka. No, I did not roofie you."

"Why?" She was slightly confused, a little intrigued, and getting a lot angry that he had the audacity to water down her drinks. She wasn't an impulsive woman who needed to be protected from herself. "Do you do that with all the women you want to help get home?"

His eyebrows went up and she hated the hint of jealousy that laced her question.

Completely serious, he said, "I don't take any women home, Cassie. At all. The club is my job, not my scene. I've wanted you since I first saw you and I didn't want you drunk, regretting your decision."

It was her turn to have her eyebrows shoot up. If he hadn't shocked her with that last sentence, she'd have embarrassed herself beaming at his proclamation.

"I'd been pretty dry in the woman department before I first saw you," he continued, "but after that, I just wanted you."

"And now what do you want?"

Chapter Three

Jace's bright eyes took on a predatory look as he sat up, drawing her gaze to the unmistakable bulge in his jeans. Her heart pounded, the beat thrumming down through her pajama pants. He looked like he wanted to devour her, spread her across the table and feast on her until they were both sated. Her body, wet and aching, was clearly ready for him, but her mind was still trying to process the whys of their discussion.

A faint musical tone caught her attention.

"My phone!" Cassie followed the sound to her foyer where she found her clothes still scattered where they were tossed last night. She located her purse, dropped right inside by the door, and dug out her phone. It was Kaitlyn calling, probably checking up on her after leaving her at the club.

"Hey, what's up?" Cassie asked, breathless, and it wasn't just from the mad dash from the kitchen. How would she discreetly field Kaitlyn's questions while Jace was still there—and then field Kaitlyn's excitement when she found out Jace was still there?

Cassie heard muffled breathing on the other end. "Cassie?" Kaitlyn squeaked into the phone.

"Yeah, is something wrong?"

"Oh God, Cassie, I need your help." Kaitlyn rushed on in a quiet voice. "We went to an abandoned building outside of town, he had a friend, we partied, then I passed out. I woke up and they were fighting. I… I think they're dead." Kaitlyn dissolved into sobs.

"Kaitlyn, where are you?" Cassie only heard her friend stifling her sobs on the other end. *Think, Dr. Stockwell!* "Where did you drive to? Did you see any signs or road names? What way out of town? Breathe, Kaitlyn. Tell me what you remember." She heard Kaitlyn trying to calm herself and breathe. "That's right, in and out, Kaitlyn. What way did you head out of town?"

"We kept heading out past the club, on one of the main roads, um… south, I think. Tyson took some off-roads to, like, an industrial place, a quarry or something, kind of abandoned. He said his friend owned the land and he knew a place we could hang. I think they're both dead, Cassie. I have no way out of here, unless I search his body for keys and I can't go back in there."

Her last words were shuttered. Kaitlyn was about to dissolve into tears again. "Breathe, Kaitlyn. Tell me where you're at now."

Kaitlyn drew in a shaky breath, "I grabbed my shit and ran out of the building. I just ran. I don't know where I'm at."

Before Kaitlyn panicked again, Cassie urged her on, "It's okay. Tell me what's around you."

"I see piles of rock and dirt. Some buildings. The one I was in was large, like a factory. I ran out, but I'm hiding behind one of the smaller buildings. I have nowhere to go, Cassie."

"Okay, Kaitlyn, you need to hang up with me and call 9-1-1, then—"

"No!"

"No," commanded a voice simultaneously from behind her. She spun around, Jace was right behind her, pulling on his boots. "We can get to her faster."

"Cassie, my phone's dying. Please help me." The phone went dead.

Cassie turned and sprinted for her room. How'd he hear the conversation?

In her room, Cassie pulled on a pair of jeans and a pink cotton tee, grabbed a pair of socks and ran to the door where Jace was waiting for her. She grabbed her shoes and purse.

"Do you still have the keys?" she asked him.

He held them up and opened the door to the garage. "I'll drive. You finish getting ready in the car."

Even as she rushed past him out the door, she took in his appearance. He was even more imposing in broad daylight. His massive size was expressed by the formfitting black button-up with the sleeves rolled up to his elbows, while the biker boots gave him an extra inch or two in height.

"We should call the police," she said, as she ran around her car to crawl into the passenger seat.

He folded himself behind the wheel and opened the garage door. "We can get to her first and they won't be able to help her."

As she buckled up, she asked, "Then what happens when we get there?"

Jace calmly drove through the streets. "You'll need to trust me. I think I know who owns property in that part of town. The police aren't going to be able to help your friend."

Cassie stared at him, confused. "Why can't they help? Wait—you know where she's at?"

"I have an idea." Jace dug his phone out of his pocket and hit speed dial while navigating through traffic. They were heading the direction of the club, presumably to follow the route Tyson took Kaitlyn.

Jace spoke quietly into the phone. Even in these close quarters, she could hardly make out any words. It sounded like he was asking his boss for directions.

Jace hung up, his attention back on the road. Ironic that here was man she had no idea what to do with less than an hour ago, and now she was extremely grateful to have him with her. How would she have found Kaitlyn otherwise? Calling the police to say her adult friend who partied with a couple of men last night was in trouble south of town didn't seem like a good start. Driving aimlessly around town wouldn't have been productive, either. She didn't have Kaitlyn's fighting skills. If she somehow happened on her wayward friend and if those men were still alive, then what? Hide behind Kaitlyn to call the police and hope her friend's black belts could save them both? Introduce herself as "Dr. Stockwell" and offer free psychoanalysis?

Jace's silence frayed Cassie's nerves. Maybe she should do what she did best and ask some questions.

"Do you know whose land it is?"

Jace shook his head. "I don't know him. I've heard of him, though."

"How bad is he?" she prompted, trying not to shout *Tell me everything you know, dammit!*

Jace's jaw clenched, "He's involved in some… dealings."

"Oh… *shit*."

"Yeah." They drove in silence a little longer. They were on the outskirts of West Creek, now having passed Pale Moonlight, which sat on the outer edge of town anyway. This part of the city wasn't as affluent as the rest. It wasn't saying much, probably why the club patrons came from a rougher crowd. The houses were further apart, a little more rundown. More trees popped up and soon the terrain got hillier and more wooded. Most of West Creek was the stereotypical wrong side of the tracks. It sat across the river from Freemont, a much larger metropolis with a more refined reputation.

Cassie sat forward, intent on the surroundings, as Jace turned off the highway onto a gravel road. Every once in a while they passed a business—

kayak and canoe rentals, small bed trucking company—until soon it was nothing but trees.

Jace slowed and turned off onto a smaller gravel road that wound down around a hillside in the direction of the river. At one time, the road had been well maintained, but as it was now, Cassie wondered how in the world the small sports car Kaitlyn had rode out in survived the jaunt. Her heart thumped when they passed large mounds of different types of rock. They'd arrived at the quarry.

Jace slowed the car as the larger building Kaitlyn mentioned came into view. He steered off the road and turned her car facing out, killing the engine.

He faced her. "I need you to stay here. Get behind the wheel, doors locked, ready to go at the first sign of trouble. I'll go look for your friend."

"I'm not waiting here," she said flatly.

"Cassie, I'm not going to ar—"

"Jace," she cut him off, "I can't sit here not knowing what's going on. I know. I have no guns, laughable self-defense skills, I get it. I'm no Jackie Chan. But I can't just sit here."

Jace stared at her for a heartbeat, two heartbeats, three… then sighed. "All right. If I scent anything that might be a threat to you, we're gone. Your safety is my main concern."

Relieved and more than a bit touched, Cassie nodded and went to open the door. Jace grabbed her arm and pulled her into him. Gently cupping her cheek he brought his mouth down to hers. Cassie instantly melted under him despite the circumstances. The gentleness he expressed through his kiss was completely unlike what his appearance and demeanor represented. Yet with her, she'd only known him to be thoughtful and protective. Meant only to be a one-night stand, here he was helping her help her best friend. No one could know what Kaitlyn meant to her. They were the odd couple. The party girl and the studious one, complete opposites, but each other's rock.

Cassie returned the kiss, greedily dancing with his tongue, wishing they were parked in the woods for a completely different reason. Just as quickly as he pulled her in, he pulled away, the look in his eyes told her he was thinking the same thing.

"Let's go," he said gruffly. He shut the door quietly and watched her get out, again having to adjust his large bulge. Images from last night of her mouth wrapped around his impressive size flooded her mind. Involuntarily, her tongue darted out to lick her bottom lip.

"Woman, you're killing me."

Startled, her eyes snapped up to his. The hunger in their depths made her feel a bit what a fuzzy little mouse must feel like when happening across a cat's path. But this mouse wouldn't mind being caught.

"Kaitlyn," she said, more to snap her focus back into place than his.

Instantly, his expression became grim. He lifted his nose into the air as if he was sniffing it. *Was he serious about scenting trouble?* She thought that was an odd phrase, not a literal one.

He began walking and held his hand out behind him, like he expected her to grab it. She jogged up, slid her hand into his large warm one, and he gently closed his around hers. Like the kiss, the intimacy of his actions were not what she expected from him.

Gravel crunched under foot. The only other sounds to be heard were rustling leaves on the trees surrounding the quarry and birds singing. It'd be an absolutely gorgeous spring day if she didn't fear for Kaitlyn's life.

Jace led them around the far side of the rock mounds to a smaller building that looked like a trailer. The head office, perhaps? It sat about a hundred yards from the larger building that must have, or may still, house the heavy equipment used in stripping the hillside.

There was a clearing between them and the trailer. Jace leaned down and spoke quietly in her ear. "Without yelling, call for Kaitlyn. She's on the other side of that building."

Curious how he'd know that, she called, "Kaitlyn?"

No answer.

"Try again," Jace said. "Only a little louder."

"Kaitlyn!"

"Ca-Cassie?"

Cassie's heart surged with relief and she wanted to sprint to her friend. "Are you all right? Stay there, we'll come to you."

"We? Who's with you?"

"Jace," Cassie paused. "The bartender."

"No police?"

Cassie desperately wanted to go to the police, but she'd calm Kaitlyn first. "No just us. We're coming to you, okay?"

Jace subtly sniffed the air again and was looking at the larger building. He jogged across the clearing, pulling her with him. They furtively searched their surroundings for any movement, and cautiously peered around the trailer to find Kaitlyn.

She sat on the ground in the dirt, with her back against the doublewide, her arms wrapped around her knees. Her dress was wrinkled and most of her makeup had worn off. Black smudges magnified the dark circles under her eyes. Dark blood stained her face and arms. Cassie rushed toward her and squatted beside her, Jace close behind.

As Cassie searched Kaitlyn's arms for injuries, but Kaitlyn shrugged her off. "It's not my blood. At least, most of it's not."

Cassie remained squatting next to the dazed girl, her hand on her shoulder. "Tell me what happened."

Kaitlyn rested her head on the wall behind her, her arms still wrapped around her knees. Her gaze flickered to Jace.

"I'll go check the building. See if, ah," Jace paused, "they're still there."

His footsteps through the gravel faded. Part of Cassie wanted to run after him and ask him to stay, she hated seeing him leave. She felt safer with him near, though they'd found Kaitlyn. Instead she sat quietly, rubbing the traumatized girl's shoulder, patiently waiting until she was ready to talk.

Kaitlyn swallowed and closed her eyes. "He drove me out here. There was this guy waiting for us. He was hot; I wanted to hook up." She turned her head to face Cassie, her expression one of such inner turmoil. Tears started streaming down her face. "I've been doing that, you know? Being with two guys at a time. When you're not with me, I've been going to the club... to The Den."

Cassie was stunned. Kaitlyn was a jelly girl? Why would she keep it a secret? She should know Cassie would support her no matter what.

"Hey," she said softly, tucking a lock of coppery hair behind Kaitlyn's ear. "It's okay. It only bothers me if it bothers you. Tell me what happened after that and don't be afraid you'll scare me off. You know I've heard worse."

A quick flash of relief crossed Kaitlyn's face, she took a deep breath. "We drank and partied—all night. Toward morning, we just kind of passed out on the bed the other guy had set up in there. He lives there. Lived, I guess." She fell quiet. Her eyes closed again, as if everything she was going to describe she could see running through her mind.

"I woke to arguing. I stayed still when I heard it was about me. Tyson was afraid that since he was at the bar with me, they'd come after him when they found my body. The other guy said they wouldn't

- 42 -

find my body. Tyson argued that I had a friend at the club who knew we left together. But he said 'you know what she is, she needs to be destroyed' and came for me.

"I was afraid he'd shoot me before I could do anything so I pretended to stretch and roll over, to face him and see how he intended to kill me. He had a knife, I pretended to panic—so I could take him off guard, right? When we fought and it was obvious I was better, and I got him to drop the knife, Tyson jumped in. He grabbed the knife and the bastard sliced me across the side. Then… then…" Kaitlyn's faced crumpled, the tears flowed harder.

Cassie murmured comforting words, her heart breaking for Kaitlyn. Her friend's wild ways had always worried her, feared they'd make her a target. But for someone to actually want her dead? Why would they hate Kaitlyn so badly they felt like they had to destroy her?

"Then," she continued after a deep breath, her voice still cracking, "I don't know what happened. It was like an out of body experience or something. My whole body felt like it was on fire, everything overly sensitive. I heard these animal sounds, like growling and snarling. I could see both of them getting taken down and shredded. But it was like I was too close to see what was killing them. Then I blacked out. I don't think for long." Kaitlyn took another deep breath. "When I came to, there was so much blood. They weren't moving. I grabbed my dress and ran out. They're dead and I think I killed them."

***

Jace walked directly to the warehouse. His heightened senses didn't pick up on anyone else in the vicinity, other than himself and the girls. Cassie would be okay with Kaitlyn, her friend would die before she would hurt her. If he hadn't seen how close the two women were in the last several months, he may have had reservations given what he recently realized about Kaitlyn.

He smelled the acrid stench of death coming from the building. He couldn't see the sports car Kaitlyn said Tyson drove. It must be inside. Walking through the open side door, Jace's vision didn't need to adjust to the dark. He saw just as well in the dark as daylight.

What was spread before him, along with what bits he'd heard from Kaitlyn's story on the phone, and what he knew her tendencies were at the club, he could make out the story of what had happened.

The warehouse had no heavy equipment stored inside. It was bare except for a corner that had been turned into sparse living quarters with a fridge, table with a hot plate and microwave, two sturdy chairs, and a bed sided by a couple of beaten down dressers. The Roadster was parked at the far end by the large garage door. Two naked bodies were spread out in between. And by spread out, Jace meant literally. Blood coated the floor and spattered the walls. A trail of organs led to one body. The other body was missing a couple of limbs. A quick scan deeper into the warehouse... oh, there they were.

Even with his past, Jace hadn't seen carnage like this before. He'd sensed the honesty in Kaitlyn's emotional turmoil. She was confused, distraught, and terrified. Was it possible a woman in her late twenties could not know what she was?

Chapter Four

The hair on Jace's arms rose the same time he sensed others in the area. He turned to sprint back to Cassie when a scream tore through the air. He ran out of the building, resisting the change that wanted to take over, unwilling to scare Cassie away before he had a chance to explain to her what he was. He sensed multiple other males in the vicinity, all like him.

He rounded the back of the trailer and skidded to a stop, before he could make a bad situation worse. Cassie was on the ground, eyes wide, panicked, with her back pressed tight to the building. Two men, dressed head to toe in black, weapons strapped all over their bodies, stood with guns pointed on a very scared, very large reddish-brown... wolf. Kaitlyn.

Her teeth bared, she snarled as she swung her head toward Jace. She didn't lunge toward him or the two men, but held her ground in front of Cassie, protecting her. She sniffed the air in Jace's direction and satisfied with what she smelled, she swung back to face to the two men, a low growl rumbling.

Jace raised his hands up to show both Kaitlyn and the men that he had no intention of any sudden movements. He knew the men, recognized them from the club, and knew what they did for a living.

"Kaitlyn," he spoke slowly, quietly. Her hearing would be extremely sensitive and overwhelmed. "Try to calm yourself. Cassie's okay. She's not hurt. These guys help our kind. They can help you understand what we are."

Kaitlyn's heaving flanks slowed. He was getting through to her. Cassie's brows drew together in confusion. He was sure she saw her friend change into the beast before her, but her mind had refused to register that the beast and Kaitlyn were one and the same.

He glanced toward the men, the one he knew as Bennett nodded almost imperceptibly. Kaitlyn growled and Jace continued. "We can help you. I won't let anyone hurt Cassie. We need you tell us what happened. You need to calm down, so you can talk to us."

Jace assumed that if Kaitlyn didn't know what she was, she wouldn't know how to transform back to her human form. If he could get her to calm down, realize neither she nor Cassie were in any immediate danger, perhaps she would turn back. Then he could get to Cassie's side and find out why the hell the Guardians were here and what the fuck he and his mate were dragged into.

"Just breathe, Kaitlyn." No one moved, all eyes were on the great red wolf before them. Werewolves, or "shifters" as they preferred to be called, were larger than the average wolf, and

Kaitlyn's back stood well above waist height. Her form filled out with lean muscle, her green eyes reflecting light from the shadow of the trailer.

The wolf's eyes dropped shut and she collapsed to the ground. Cassie gasped and backed up further, watching as red fur transformed to smooth, creamy skin and long auburn hair. Kaitlyn, lay there, out cold.

Seeing her friend passed out in front of her encouraged Cassie to peel herself off the wall and scramble forward, regardless that the strange men still had guns drawn. She leaned over Kaitlyn and shook her shoulders gently. "Kaitlyn? Are you okay? Hey, wake up." She gently moved the hair off the unconscious woman's face, hoping she'd come to.

Jace approached Cassie, her roiling emotions driving his own inner beast to the surface seeking to protect her. Bennett aimed his weapon at Jace, but that didn't stop him. He glared at Bennett. "Don't try to keep me from her."

The other man, the one called Mercury, asked, "Which one's yours, the human or the shifter?"

Cassie looked up at Jace kneeling down between her and the guns the men had trained on his back, fear and confusion staining her features.

"What's going on? What just happened?" Her voice, shaky at the beginning, got stronger. "Who are those guys?"

"They're protectors of our people. They'll want to talk to us. Help Kaitlyn."

"I've seen them before at the club." She looked over his shoulder, distrust in her eyes. The two Guardians remained still, letting the situation play out before taking any action. She looked back at him, the look of distrust remained. "What did they mean human or shifter?"

Petty as it was, he wanted to growl and snarl at Mercury and Bennett. She'd noticed them at the club. Of course, she did. All the women did. He'd had to put up seeing her with her ex, he didn't need her to notice anyone else.

"You're the human, Kaitlyn's the shifter. As you saw, she's what you'd know as a werewolf." He paused to gauge her reaction, debating on whether to confess his genetic makeup now, also.

"Werewolves aren't..." She caught herself, unable deny what she witnessed. She looked at Kaitlyn, the concern for her friend returning, processing the events of the last several minutes.

Kaitlyn moaned. "I think she's coming around," Cassie said. "We need to cover her up."

"Don't worry on our account," Bennett drawled from behind him, "nudity doesn't bother our kind much. In fact, we prefer it."

"Well, I don't want her nude around you," Cassie snapped.

"Nothing we haven't seen before," muttered Mercury.

Jace shot him a dark look knowing full well Mercury had seen plenty of Kaitlyn before. Bennett, too. At the same time. He hoped Cassie hadn't heard, but she was reaching over to pick up Kaitlyn's dress. It'd been ripped off in the transformation.

"This is no good," she decided. "I have blankets from winter in my car. We can use one of those." She looked expectantly at him.

Remaining kneeling in front of her, he dug her keys out. "Heads up!" Without looking, he threw them behind him toward Mercury. "Why don't you go grab the blanket."

Mercury snagged the keys out of the air. "What the fuck, dude?"

"I'm not leaving them. And it'd be better if there were less of you around when she wakes fully up." He nodded toward Kaitlyn who was groaning, her eyes rolling around behind her lids, her fingers starting to twitch. "She knows I'm not a threat."

Bennett lowered his weapon, but didn't holster it. "Go ahead, Mercury. I don't want her shifting again and if the blanket helps, we'd better have it. I'll radio the commander and let him know we'll meet him where their car's at when she's fully with it."

Mercury slipped his weapon, a tranq gun from what Jace could tell, back into its spot on his hip. The thickset man stalked away glaring at Jace, his dark eyes reflecting like a pool of molten iron, until he was almost out of sight. Right before he turned around the corner of the trailer, he flipped Jace the bird, who just smirked. Dickhead.

Bennett snorted at the brief exchange and spoke quietly into his radio comm, and Cassie rubbed Kaitlyn's shoulder. *To comfort her friend or herself?*

"Are they human or shifter?" Cassie asked quietly.

"Shifter," Jace said, dreading her next question.

"And you? Human or shifter."

"Shifter."

Paling, Cassie nodded, avoiding his gaze. Did she believe at all what she saw, what he just told her? She opened her mouth to say something, but Kaitlyn moaned and opened her eyes.

"Cassie? What happened?" As the memories flooded back, Kaitlyn sat up quickly, noticed she was naked, and there were still others around besides Cassie, and curled in on herself. "I didn't kill anyone again, did I?" she whispered.

Cassie shook her head and Mercury came around the corner carrying a blanket with floral designs that seemed absurd in this situation. Jace was afraid she would shift seeing him again, but guessed that since this time he was holding a granny blanket instead of a tranq gun, that sat better with her.

Mercury dropped the blanket to her lap. "Cover up and let's go."

Cassie wrapped the blanket around her and then helped her stand. Jace hovered, wanting to help his mate out, but unwilling to touch any section of Kaitlyn's bare body.

"Let's go back to the car and get you home," Cassie murmured to Kaitlyn.

"Y'all aren't going home. You need to come with us," Bennett said.

"Where the fuck do you think you're taking them?" Jace growled.

"Where the fuck we say we're going," Mercury replied, smugly.

"We'll take them, and you, to the compound for questioning. We're going to need to talk to them both. And this is your warning, Miller," Bennett said, calling Jace by his last name. "We'll let you stay with your woman, but if you cause any problems, we'll knock you out." He patted the gun he'd just holstered.

Mercury grinned, resting his hand on the tranq gun strapped to his side.

"You do anything more than chat with her, I'll tear you and your compound apart," Jace threatened.

Mercury barked out a laugh. "What's wrong, Miller? Afraid it'll remind you of prison?"

Jace's heart stopped. *Motherfucker!* Cassie's jaw dropped, Kaitlyn looked questioningly at him, her curiosity at the sudden turn of conversation momentarily distracting her from the men with guns and passing out naked.

Cassie's arms wrapped protectively around Kaitlyn, who clutched the blanket closely around her. Cassie had recovered from the prison announcement and Jace would bet she was regretting who she let drive her home last night. She and Kaitlyn began a slow walk in the direction of her car. Jace and the other two men moved along at the same speed.

"Let me talk with Cassie first. And I'll be with her when you talk with her," he told Bennett.

Bennett, always the more easygoing one, shrugged and said, "Not up to me, Miller, but I'll pass on your request to Commander Fitzsimmons."

Rhys Fitzsimmons was the Guardian pack commander for the West Creek area. Jace didn't know how the Guardians divided themselves up geographically, but each major pack area had its own Lycan Guardian pack assigned to protect the shifters and their secrets. Jace knew the commander from the club. The Guardians hung out there on their downtime. It was a good place to keep up on pack gossip, catch wind of anything that might be going down, and fulfill the increased sexual needs unmated Guardians had. The last part excluded the commander. Jace only knew him as all business, all the time.

That's all Jace could do for now. Hope the Guardians would let him talk with Cassie first. Hope she'd listen. But he'd die before he left her side.

***

Cassie walked slowly next to Kaitlyn as she picked her way barefoot over the rocks and gravel.

They were almost to her Honda, following the big guy, Mercury. Cassie mentally snorted. All three men were big. But Mercury, though not quite as tall, was wider than the other two with a large muscular back and a V-taper most men would envy. His looks fit his name, if that was his real name. He was still over six feet tall, with a short military haircut. His hair was almost black but when light reflected off it, it looked…well, like mercury. His eyes were so dark they also looked black. But when Jace pissed him off, they changed. Like a cat's eyes in the dark, the reflected light gave them a shine… again, like mercury. Like Jace, Mercury wasn't classically handsome, but the rugged manliness of his features emanated raw sensuality, she bet he was like catnip for women. Well, she actually knew that for a fact since she'd seen him heading into a room back in The Den, the one all the jelly girls came from.

The thought of Jace led her back down a path she wasn't sure her mind was ready to travel. His presence was comforting, disconcerting, arousing, and even more disconcerting that it was arousing. So she'd brought an ex-con home. She'd wait and reserve judgment until she found out what he did time for. He might be like Martha Stewart, a little insider trading, for all she knew. She'd sat across from a few sociopaths in her short career, digging around their minds, and her gut didn't tell her Jace was mentally unstable and volatile. Since he started pouring drinks for her last night, he'd been thoughtful and protective. He was supposed to be a one-nighter to boost her damaged ego, her walk on the wild side. She would have never had a second thought that she wasn't the same to him, except maybe his walk was on the extremely tame side. After their talk in her kitchen, and then back behind that trailer where he'd made it clear to the Guardians she was his, she wasn't sure what he was to her.

Her mind finished working through what was normal about her current situation and now it settled on the large, red wolf that was Kaitlyn. The change happened so fast, and she'd been distracted by the men quietly appearing, seemingly out of nowhere, she feared Kaitlyn disappeared and was afraid of the giant beast snarling in front of her. But she saw every nanosecond when the wolf transitioned back into Kaitlyn. As much as she'd like to tell herself it wasn't real, between what the guys were saying, and Kaitlyn's story, there was only so much she could deny.

"Hold up," the other Guardian said when they reached her car. "We'll wait for the commander."

With perfect timing, the commander came strolling out of the warehouse. Even from a distance, he was a man who commanded respect and demanded obedience. He was even taller than his two teammates, almost as broad as Mercury, and to say he had a stern expression would have been an understatement. He had reddish-blond hair, but it was trimmed close to the scalp like Mercury's, not kept longer so it could be tousled stylishly like the other Guardian wore his, the one whose name she didn't know. No, Cassie was sure there was nothing frivolous about this man. The commander walked with such power and assurance, with the air of ultimate authority, there was no mistaking who was in charge.

As he approached, Jace crowded closer behind her, always protective. His presence was welcome since the approach of Commander Fitzsimmons made her realize that her wishes about what happened next were not in her hands. Sure, she could run but how far would she get? She was fast, but she only had two legs. She was at the mercy of these men now and it wasn't only her future at risk, it was Kaitlyn's, too. She'd known Kaitlyn half her life. They were so close she thought she knew everything about her. She was pretty sure her friend would've mentioned, "Hey, this one time, I turned into a big fucking wolf."

"Bennett," Commander Fitzsimmons said when he got closer, "you and Mercury use the car to take the ladies back to the compound."

Cassie felt, and the same time heard, the low rumble from behind her.

"I stay with Cassie," Jace demanded. "She's mine."

The commander's eyes flicked back and forth between her and Jace, and he subtly lifted his nose like he was catching a whiff of something. Of course he was a shifter, too, and Jace really had been scenting for trouble when they'd first arrived.

What the commander was scenting now, she wasn't sure, as she was apparently the oddball human in this group.

"And, I'm not leaving Kaitlyn." Cassie chimed in, unwilling to leave her friend alone with armed men.

Commander Fitzsimmons raised an eyebrow. "Mr. Miller, do you plan to cause any problems for Bennett on the way to our facilities?"

"Only if you plan on hurting her in any way. And hurting Kaitlyn would hurt her."

"Miss Savoy," Commander Fitzsimmons turned his intense hazel stare to Kaitlyn, "do you plan on disrupting the trip to our facilities?"

All heads turned to Kaitlyn. She met his stare boldly, thinking for a bit. "What are your plans for me?"

"Miss Savoy, we'd only like to talk." The commander's voice was gentler than he used on Jace. "And to help you. It's… unusual for one of our kind to go unknown and unnoticed, unshifted for so long. We will teach you."

"And the men in there," Kaitlyn nodded toward the warehouse, "I killed them, right?"

Commander Fitzsimmons nodded.

She paused, letting the confirmation sink in. "What will you do to me for that?"

"Those men were going to kill you. Probably torture you first for information. They do that to our kind—hunt us. As far I'm concerned, you saved yourself and saved us some work. Mercury and I will stay, and take care of them."

"Why'd they want to kill me?" Kaitlyn asked.

"Allow us to escort you and your friends to the safety of our facility so we can fill you in."

Kaitlyn glanced at Cassie who just shrugged. Their only choice was between running and fighting. Kaitlyn was a superb fighter, and Cassie loved to run, but against these men, neither woman could fight nor run to freedom. To Cassie's trained eye, the commander was genuine and the other two hadn't hurt them yet. Cassie wanted answers about Kaitlyn and Jace, and this was the less violent way.

"Mr. Miller, you drive. Bennett will give you the directions." With that, the commander turned and strode back to the warehouse, making not a sound. Mercury silently followed.

Chapter Five

The Guardian headquarters was an impressive compound tucked away deep in the woods. Anyone who happened upon it would think an eccentric millionaire built out here for privacy. The main two-story building was a cross between old-world mansion and rustic cabin, built from a combination of log and rock on the exterior. The center was a giant A-frame with enormous windows looking out into the woods. Cassie was blown away by the grandeur of the estate.

Large cottonwoods were spread throughout the property as if the log mansion and the accompanying buildings were built around them. A log-built garage connected the dwelling by an intricate breezeway that could be open to the elements or closed during the winter months. Behind those, there was more, much more, but she could not make any of it out past the main house. From what she did see, there appeared to be smaller more rustic cabins scattered in the hills around the primary property.

It'd been a quiet trip. Other than Bennett's driving instructions, no one said a word. What would be the point to ask questions? She couldn't talk to Kaitlyn privately, she wanted to hear Jace's story without an audience, and she doubted Bennett would answer anything. So she stared out the window, trying to ignore the heat of Jace's body next to her in the tiny car. If she turned to look at her ex-con sitting there, dangerously handsome, she'd start seeing images of him naked and not care what he'd done to spend time in prison.

The drive took well over an hour and she suspected that Bennett took them through several unnecessary twists and turns. She'd tried to memorize the way, but soon gave up. All she knew was that they were still south of West Creek and hadn't crossed the river. Some of the roads they took, she had no idea they'd been there until Jace turned onto them.

Nervous about the hidden, top-secret world she was entering, Cassie jumped when Jace softly put a hand on the small of her back as she got out of the car. How'd he move so fast? Reluctant to leave Kaitlyn's side, her friend gave her a small smile as she climbed out and shut her door, blanket still wrapped tightly around her. Cassie didn't look at Jace as he walked by her side to the majestic building in front of them. She felt safer with him next to her, in his warmth, but didn't trust she wouldn't take one look at him and jump into his arms, and didn't trust that his arms were the safest place for her.

His hand hot on her back, the walk up to the doors had her stomach fluttering. This was it. What was going to happen to her? Were there more Guardians waiting to haul her off for questioning? Were they waiting to attack her and Kaitlyn in the privacy of their lodge? The massive wooden door opened and they stepped in.

***

Jace sensed the tension building in Cassie as they walked into Guardian headquarters. She avoided him as much as she could. It stung but he refused to let her run from him, physically or mentally. He made sure he kept physical contact with her as often as possible. When they crossed the threshold into the house, she stopped. He gently pulled her off to the side so Bennett and Kaitlyn could enter.

"It's empty," Cassie muttered.

"Not quite." The male voice came from their right. She jumped. No one else moved, they'd been able to sense the new shifter once they entered, but Cassie's human senses couldn't pick him up.

"Sorry to startle you, Dr. Stockwell." The man came out of the hallway into view. He was another Guardian, wearing the same type of tactical clothes, but not as loaded down with gear. He was older, his salt-and-pepper hair in the same short military cut most the Guardians seemed to prefer. "I'm Master Bellamy. Commander Fitzsimmons called ahead and explained the situation. I'd like to lead Miss Savoy to the locker room where she can clean up and get into some clothes before I talk with her. Bennett, take the other two to talk. I hear Dr. Stockwell needs to catch up before we discuss current events."

"Yes, sir." Bennett nodded, exchanged a knowing look with Master Bellamy, and started toward the stairs.

"Wait!" Cassie exclaimed. "I'm staying with Kaitlyn."

"It's okay, Cassie," Kaitlyn reassured her. "I'll be fine and Jace will be with you."

Cassie's expression said Jace's presence wasn't reassuring to her. Jace forced himself to remain calm, Cassie was still here with him, hadn't panicked after all she'd seen. Despite their difference in titles, hers of "doctor" and his of "ex-con," he would win her. He had to; she belonged to him. His hand on her lower back, he gently urged her to follow Bennett.

There was little by way of decoration in the place. It didn't need any, the skylights and large front windows lit up every corner, highlighting the natural beauty of the logs and decorative rock. Even the mortar used to place the stone was uniquely colored to blend with the elements; it was a work of art. It didn't surprise Jace that the Guardian compound would be built from nature, into nature, by those who were intimately familiar with living off the land itself.

They followed Bennett down the wide hallway with large doors on each side. Each door had an electronic reader on the outside allowing only secure access. Jace didn't see any on the main door they entered, but there had to be some type of security. The Guardians wouldn't let just anyone walk in.

Bennett stopped and put his thumb on the reader by the first door on the right. It unlocked with a muffled *thunk* and swung open to display a modern, sterile interrogation room, much like one he'd been in before going to prison. The contemporary room was in stark contrast to the rest of the rustic manor. Jace could only guess what the rest of the lodge hid inside, given what the Guardians sometimes had to do to protect their species.

"You two head on in and have your little chat. I'll be in to talk with Dr. Stockwell when you're done," Bennett said.

Cassie stalled at the doorway, reluctantly wandering inside.

Jace started in, then turned back to Bennett. "You're going to listen to everything, aren't you?"

Bennett flashed a wicked grin as he left.

"Asshole." Jace growled quietly as the door shut out Bennett's chuckle.

Cassie sat behind the table in one of the metal chairs. She folded her arms and glared at the wall. If that look she was giving the wall had been turned on him, Jace was sure he'd be reduced to a pile of dust.

He quietly pulled out the chair next to her, turned it facing her and sat down. He could hear her breathing hitch faster, his eyes wandered down to her breasts, shoved up by her arms folded under them. His desire flared as he remembered exactly what they looked like. He wondered what color bra she put on, if it cupped and held her, like he had last night. His hand itched to trace its outline under her shirt.

"Well?" she said tersely. She'd crossed her legs and the top leg bounced rhythmically. It was her only movement otherwise. "Quit looking at my chest and talk. I won't interrupt. I'll save my questions until you're done, cuz I'm sure I'll have a few."

Now that Jace found himself exactly where he wanted to be, other than nestled between her soft thighs, he had no idea where to start. He'd rehearsed this conversation in his head countless times, like a fifteen-year-old boy planning to declare his love might practice in the mirror. At least his voice wouldn't, *shouldn't*, crack and he wasn't covered in post-puberty zits.

"Start at the beginning," Cassie said, as if she knew the reason for his hesitation.

The beginning... okay. When he first saw her? No. His childhood. No, that wouldn't do. His parents? Yep. Aren't parental issues always a good place to start explaining why life got a little fucked up? And he still had the whole "I turn into a wolf" thing to talk about, too.

"My mom wanted to raise us like a normal family," he began. "A normal *human* family. Some shifters live in colonies, hidden in the woods like this place. They can be freer with their lives, not live in so much secrecy.

"My mom and dad met in a colony called Great Moon where they grew up together and stayed after they mated to raise a family. But Agents, sadistic humans and vampires who hunt our kind, found the colony…" Jace drifted off, old memories threatening to take over—distant screams, his mom calling for his dad… "They almost destroyed it. But they didn't. The wolves were too strong for them, but we lost a lot of our own, including my dad and brother. He was older than me, Keve. He'd been through his first transition so he could fight. Mom hid me and Mage, my little sister, and defended the house. I was nine, Mage was four."

Jace dropped his head and his gaze hit the floor. He thought he had worked through his past during his years behind bars. He sure had a hell of a lot of thinking time. But talking about it again came dangerously close to reliving it. He could feel Cassie looking at him, no longer glaring at the wall.

"After that," he continued, "Mom wanted to integrate with humans as much as possible. She did all she could to blend: adopted a mainstream surname, got a job, put us in public school. We were completely cut off from everything about our heritage. My first transition was something I endured. It was the only time we went to the woods, and then pretended it never happened.

"We lived in a bad part of town. Some colonies are pretty progressive, have a lot of tech and investments. Not Great Moon. We left with next to nothing and stayed that way. I protected Maggie, watched out for her at school and when she started working at a diner. One day, I was waiting in the parking lot for her to get off work when I noticed this guy hanging around. I'd noticed him before. His vibe was creepy, man. I mean, *creepy*. I think they coined the term just for him. He was older and the way he looked at Maggie... I knew he was bad news. I tried to dissuade him from ever being interested in her." And he had, but even Jace's special power of influence did nothing to lessen the obsession the stranger had for his sister.

"He was there every day, waiting for Maggie. Sometimes he'd talk with her, sit in her section so she had to serve him. She was only fifteen. He was in his forties. Even when I couldn't see him, I could feel him there.

"One day, my bike got a flat and I was late to pick her up. She closed the diner that night and when she locked up there was nowhere to go. He got her." By now, Cassie had turned in her chair facing him, hands folded on her lap, their knees an inch apart. He wanted to haul her to him, nuzzle into her neck, and forget the past and present.

"I pulled up in time to see his car drive off. The diner was dark and Maggie was nowhere. *Nowhere*. I tried to follow him but he was gone.

"I knew where he lived, though. Maggie got the information for me off of his credit card one time when he paid, and I got everything I could on him. I went to his house in this fancy little part of Freemont. His car was in the drive so I broke in. But he didn't hear me. He was in the basement with Maggie." Jace stopped. Explaining the shifter bit wasn't nearly as difficult as what was coming up.

"She was unconscious. He had tied her to a four-poster bed and was undressing her. I don't know how I managed to stay human when I beat the shit out of him. I was about to untie Maggie and call the police when the bastard started laughing. Laughing! He said, 'They'll never believe you, you filthy piece of trash. I'll tell them she was obsessed with me. That she broke into my house to get close to me. Who do you think they'll listen to? Two street kids? Or a high-powered attorney?'"

Jace paused, staring at the floor, elbows resting on his thighs. He wasn't seeing the floor, he was seeing everything that had happened.

"When I ripped him off Maggie and threw him to the ground, he knocked over the end table and some papers spilled all over the floor. I was trying to figure out what to do when I saw what the papers were."

Cassie still hadn't moved, keeping her promise to not interrupt. What kind of doctor was she, to remain patient and not interject with questions while his memories threatened to overtake him?

"They were photos… of girls like Maggie—young, long dark hair, naked, tied to a bed. They appeared dead, their bodies battered. I knew he got away with it all and he was right. He'd get away with kidnapping Maggie. Maybe even try to finish the job another time. He had to be stopped. It all had to end, so I finished him."

Cassie seemed to quit breathing. Then she folded her arms across her chest again. Her knee brushed his as she re-crossed her legs. He waited for her to get up and ask that one of them be removed from the room. He waited for her to cry *You're a murderer?* And yes, he was.

"Go on," she said. She was still looking at him. He hung onto that and looked up. She was guarded, but not disgusted or hostile. His head was even with hers since he was hunched over, elbows on thighs. He gazed into her warm brown eyes, the rest of his story was easy, except for the unknown ending of what she'd do.

"His family came after me with their legal team. Blamed me for the girls, for his death, everything. I pleaded guilty to the lesser charge of manslaughter and got eight years in prison and two years probation. My mom cut me off, my *sister* even cut me off. I brought attention to our family when Mom sacrificed everything to hide us in plain sight. Even the wolves wanted nothing to do with me, I might bring attention to our species.

"Commander Fitzsimmons came to talk to me in jail before my sentencing. All he said was 'Human crime, human time. We have someone on the inside; you lose it in there we'll put you down.'

"I did my time, got out, and got a job at Pale Moonlight. Christian's a pack leader, takes in poor fucks like me who have no one and nowhere to go. Then you walked in, Cassie."

She held her arms tighter, her crossed leg started bobbing again.

"I saw you and knew you were mine."

Cassie ceased all movement, the rest of his story temporarily forgotten. Was he kidding? What did he mean she was his? He was sitting there, dressed head-to-toe in black with his shaved head, piercing eyes, and boots that screamed "my other car is a Harley." He worked in a bar with bombshells showing off their artillery. Constantly. All. Night. Long. She was pretty secure and didn't feel like she lost out in the looks department. She liked her shower-and-go hair and, with a wicked running habit, she enjoyed her desserts enough that she didn't lean out too badly and lose her T&A. But for this guy to call her *his*? Like they were destined to be together?

"But you were with that guy," Jace bit off the word, interrupting her thoughts. "I knew you were out of my league – the way you moved, the way you dressed, fuck, even your ex screamed class. I decided to wait. You'd realize he was wrong, you'd be drawn back to the club, we'd be together. I was impulsive once. I lost my life and my family. I wasn't going to make the same mistake with you. So I waited." Jace shrugged, as if it was the most logical thing in the world. Except she knew differently, practically seeing lightning rods of tension course through him.

She continued to stare at him. Her leg twitched again.

"Ask me anything," Jace prodded.

"Are you saying you saw me and it was love at first sight?" she asked incredulously.

"We mate for life. You're my mate."

The leg stopped bobbing again. "And this wolf stuff. It's real?"

"Yep."

Cassie took a deep "so help me" breath and tilted her head back to look at the ceiling. *Dr. Stockwell, you are not allowed to lose your shit.*

"But I'm human," she said, feeling slightly absurd for having to make a point of it.

"Cassie, look at me," Jace said.

She did. He reached forward and grasped her hands. His fingers brushed her breasts as he did so, making them sensitive and heavy. How did he still have that effect on her? Confessing that he wasn't human, murdered someone, that she was his, and she got turned on when he brushed her breasts?

"We sense our mates, shifter or human, when we meet them. Human mates aren't unusual but they aren't common. We can spend decades looking for our mate, hoping we'll be drawn together."

WTF, did he just say decades?

He was so earnest, so sincere, and after all he told her, all she wanted to know was about the whole mate thing. "And what does mate mean exactly, in the werewolf world?"

"Shifters," he corrected. "We are linked. For life. And Cassie, we live longer than humans." He stopped to let that sink in.

"How much longer?"

A bit reluctantly, he said, "Centuries."

"*What?*"

"As a human, when you bind with me, you'd share my lifespan."

"Share lifespans," she echoed, her mind reeling. Her rational mind argued with her buzzing emotions.

Abruptly, she stood up, dropping his hands, losing the warmth of his body, and paced at the end of the table in the tiny room. He stood slowly, but didn't move toward her.

"Look, Jace, this is all," she gestured all around her, "a lot. I need some time, room to breathe."

"Cassie, I—,"

"You need to go." She kept pacing, hands on hips. "No, you know what? I need to go. Where's Kaitlyn?" She walked to the door and tried to open it, but they were locked in. She banged on it with her palm.

"Bennett!" Cassie called through the door. "Open up. I want to talk to Kaitlyn."

She was about to pound again when the door swung open. She jumped back.

Bennett walked in. "Jace, you wanna give us a minute? I'd like to chat with Dr. Stockwell before I take her home."

"Where's Kaitlyn?" Cassie demanded.

"She's talking to Master Bellamy. Jace, wait in the hall."

"I'm not fucking leaving," Jace said. He squared off with Bennett. The fair-haired man was only an inch shorter than Jace and not the least bit intimidated.

Cassie resumed pacing.

"Look man, give her some room," Bennett said quietly. "I'm not going to hurt her. You know my life is protecting our people, including human mates."

Cassie could just make out what he was saying. Some of the tension eased in the tiny interrogation room. She needed to learn about all of this world, find Kaitlyn, and with Jace next her, all she could think about was the word "mating." When she heard that word, she remembered what his naked skin felt like on hers and wanted more.

"I'm okay, Jace. Please wait in the hall for me. I'm sure it won't take long." She hoped she hit on his major concerns and he didn't argue.

Hurt flashed across his handsome features and was gone just as quickly. He turned to leave and

Cassie yearned to go after him, suddenly not wanting to be alone in the room with the other male, craving only to be by Jace's side. But she needed answers.

"Leave the door cracked," Jace muttered.

***

"Dr. Stockwell, please have a seat."

"Unless you're my patient, it's just Cassie." *Unless you're me. I call myself Dr. Stockwell all the time*. Especially when crazy happened—like when a patient breaks down mid-session and breaks her office window trying to escape when she was having him committed. Or when her best friend kills two people, then her BFF and the one night stand end up being werewolves. That's full "Dr. Stockwell" territory.

"Cassie it is." He pulled up a chair on the other side of the table. She sat back down in her chair, crossed her ankles, and folded her hands in front of her on the table. *Okay, Dr. Stockwell, get your shit back together.*

"We'd like to talk with you about Kaitlyn."

"You'll have to ask Kaitlyn about Kaitlyn."

"Cassie, we want to help her."

"Look Bennett, if she wants you to help her, she'll let you. Other than that, Kaitlyn's life isn't mine to talk about."

Bennett sat quiet for a while. Then he crossed his arms and leaned back in his chair. "Just one question, then. Have you ever seen her shift?"

Cassie barked out a laugh. "That would be no. I knew nothing about werewolves or shifters or whatever you call yourselves, until today."

Bennett studied her. She studied him back. He was a real showstopper, with his dirty blond hair expertly tousled to look messy-chic and his dark blue bedroom eyes. His face, with smooth flawless skin, high cheekbones, and strong jaw, could look easygoing and friendly, as it did now, or hard and ruthless like back at the quarry when she first saw him.

Black cargos seemed to be the team's uniform with a black shirt that stretched across his broad shoulders, chest, and biceps. He no doubt had washboard abs like a gym rat hooked on protein shakes. The amount of weapons strapped between shoulders and ankles definitely led to the "don't fuck with me, but I'll fuck you" appeal.

Yet for all his masculine appeal, he didn't do it for her. She felt no stomach flutters, no inclination to flirt (like she ever did), and no breathlessness when she looked at his handsome face. All of that happened only when she thought of Jace, and he didn't have to be in the building.

Bennett's lips spread in a sympathetic smile, his eyes crinkling at the corners. "Gave you quite a shock, I imagine. You handled yourself well, staying calm, keeping quiet."

Cassie nodded, encouraging the praise. It was Psych 101—sympathize and acknowledge the subject's feelings, and she wanted to see what angle he was playing. He searched for information, but was it to help Kaitlyn, or use against her? Cassie wanted information, but instinctively knew Bennett didn't plan on sharing.

"I suppose you got pretty street savvy once you became part of the system, going into foster care. You and Kaitlyn bonded pretty tightly, each with your own tragedy so you could understand each other."

Did he really think this was going to work? She nodded again.

"You fostered with her family, right? Her adoptive parents hoping an intelligent, mature girl could mentor Kaitlyn through the teenage years, which are rough enough for girls who haven't lost their loved ones in unimaginable ways." Bennett folded his hands on the table, leaning slightly forward like she was. He lost the smile, but kept the sympathy in his eyes.

The situation was absurd. Here was a guy, strapped head to toe with knives, more probably where she couldn't see, at least two guns, *and are those throwing stars?* and he's trying to Dr. Phil her into telling him about Kaitlyn.

There was nothing to tell. They seemed to know the two girls' history together but unless they wanted to hear about first heartbreaks and embarrassing tampon stories, she didn't know what they were looking for and she wouldn't tell them if she did. She and Kaitlyn bonded over their past tragedies, beyond that they were normal women who had each other's backs. They could ask Kaitlyn about her past. Good luck with that.

"I don't know what to tell you," Cassie said, "unless you want to hear about the time the cops were called to a frat party when we were nineteen and we both bailed out of the window onto thorny rose bushes. It hurt, but we got away. The whole thing was a real pain the ass," she deadpanned.

Bennett laughed with her. The sympathy replaced by determination.

"Cassie, help us understand how an adult shifter can live without transitioning, without anyone seeing her shift or knowing anything about her parentage."

The hormones were ramping down with Jace out of the room, the adrenaline from the morning had worn off, and breakfast had burned off long ago. Hungry, tired, and pretty fucking irritated at the way Bennett was trying to play her—this is what she did for a living, dammit!—she sat forward a little more.

"Bennett, you seem cool—when you want to. You seem like you want to be my friend, someone safe in the land of big, bad wolves, someone I can tell my secrets to—if I had any. I bet you're the responsible one, second-in-command it appears. You want to be seen as easygoing, dedicated, dependable. Am I right?"

Not waiting for an answer, she continued, "But don't forget, Bennett, I've seen you at the club, coming out of the dark hallway, turning that country boy smile onto a woman looking for attention. I've seen your face after she takes the bait. It's not delight. I've seen your face as you pass the jelly girl off to her friends after you're done with her. It's not satisfaction. Even more, I've seen you when you weren't in The Den, sitting at the bar nursing a warm beer, lost in thought. If you were human, do you know what I'd think? That you're broken inside."

Bennett's face lost all color, fading to a shade that could have been cut from stone.

"Someone destroyed you and you haven't recovered," Cassie said. "You're all duct tape and super glue, being what everyone wants and expects you to be. Inside though, you're falling apart. Worried how much longer you can do it and what happens when you can't anymore. I'm here, if you want to talk. Otherwise, I, one, don't know anything and, two, wouldn't tell you anyway."

Silence.

Finally, Bennett ran a hand through his hair and stood. Walking to the door he held it open for her.

"Why don't we see what's going on with your friend."

Chapter Six

Kaitlyn felt human after her shower. But that was only temporary as she remembered that she may, in fact, not be as human as she thought. She hated lying to her friend, seemed like she'd been doing it for months. Lying by omission, if anything. She told Cassie everything, they were closer than sisters. Since Cassie spent her days listening to mental patients talk about their deepest secrets Kaitlyn was safe from any judgment for the way she lived her life. Lately, the pressure building in her each month, the need for extreme intercourse to release it, it wasn't something she wanted to face herself, much less unload on her BFF. The last couple of months, she released it and crossed her fingers that was it, end of story. Until the uneasiness inside started again, like having butterflies, until it became so uncomfortable she could hardly walk. The worst case of lady blue balls, on steroids, times ten.

She didn't exactly lie to Cassie when she relayed events from earlier this morning. And it wasn't as if Cassie didn't find out eventually about the main event Kaitlyn had left out of her story; that she felt her transformation, every millisecond, when she turned and killed those men. She was aware that she became a wolf even though she didn't have a mirror to confirm. Flowing into another form was exhilarating, an awakening, like the most natural move in the world. Ripping into bodies matched the rush of her shift. The acrid blood tainting her taste buds should disgust her. She didn't want to know what it said about her that it didn't.

The transformation sparked vague memories. Images from past nightmares that she always chalked up to being just that—nightmares. Kaitlyn spent the morning hiding from those images more than the memory of the two men she ripped apart early this morning. The guys were convenient and it wasn't until it was almost permanently too late that she sensed any danger from them. Up until that point, it'd been raging hormones and sexual need, and the temporary fulfillment that would only last days to weeks. She should feel torn up about those men, wonder if they had family. She *killed*, but remorse remained an unattainable emotion. Her intuition screamed that if she hadn't destroyed them, they would've kept hunting women. Despite her lack of regret, she wasn't ready to pat herself on the back. She didn't just kill them, she'd decimated them.

Kaitlyn switched her disturbing train of thought from translating the images and possible memories from her past and inexplicable killing instincts to dwelling on her guilt about Cassie. She started dragging her to Pale Moonlight to check the place out after she heard about The Den from one of her martial arts clients. It had taken several visits before she mustered up the courage to actually participate in Den festivities. But she'd taken to ditching Cassie to leave with a candidate to help her release. It was unlike her. Not being known for being traditionally responsible as a grown young lady, she'd never taken chances with her body and well-being. Having a good time, dancing on bars? Yes. The occasional police call to get bailed out when she couldn't flirt her way out of public intoxication? Yes, but that was totally unjustified since it was a street dance. But driving off with unknown men, not just for a quick lay, but to hunker down somewhere and get it on for hours. Every time she ditched Cassie, she didn't end up with her clothes off and that somehow helped her feel less guilty. Cassie wised up and started bringing Grant when Kaitlyn asked her to the club.

Kaitlyn couldn't help the groan when Grant came to mind. He was a good guy. Anyone would be lucky to pair up with that one. He was good-looking and he tolerated Kaitlyn and her behavior around Cassie. He was just so *nice*. And that was the problem. Kaitlyn wanted more than nice for Cassie. She needed someone who'd bring her out of the safe, comfy life she'd built for herself. Her predictable, quiet, uneventful life. They used to stay up all night talking about what they'd do once they turned eighteen, had a diploma, and were free to go anywhere and do anything. Kaitlyn was still trying to figure out what anywhere and anything was, but it sure didn't include settling down and working Monday through Friday, nine-to-five. Her foster sister might have thought that was what she desired most in life, but Kaitlyn knew it was wrong for both of them.

To help stave off her conscience when her life started to jumble up into a hot mess, Kaitlyn threw herself into her maid of honor duties for the upcoming nuptials. It wasn't enough to payback her friendship and now it was all for nothing. When Cassie called her last night, upset and in disbelief that Grant called everything off, Kaitlyn played the part of sympathetic friend and talked her out of the house to go to the club.

Then she hung up and danced around.

But yet again, even before walking into the club last night, the urge got to be too much. Tyson had a fast car, a friend, and privacy. Entering the world of shitty BFF again, she dreaded leaving Cassie. Until she saw how the bartender looked at her. She knew her friend was oblivious to Jace's interest. Kaitlyn had been to Pale Moonlight enough to know that while the staff may not overtly fraternize, they kept any sexual escapades with their clientele on the downlow, heavily utilized The Den and only chose any who were also looking for quick, forgettable hookups.

But not Jace. Kaitlyn noticed him only because he looked through anyone at the club. He watched for empty glasses to refill, customers needing service, and trouble brewing. He didn't watch the bountiful breasts on display. He never noticed the women with short skirts and sprayed on pants who *accidently* dropped something in front of the bar. Kaitlyn saw some bend over shows put on that would make any strip club ask for lessons. Kaitlyn's first thought was that he was gay, but nope, men didn't turn his head either.

The only thing that turned his head was Cassie. And the look he saved for Grant when he thought no one would see… that man was into her friend something fierce. Kaitlyn would've fueled that fire, but Cassie had too much respect and loyalty for Grant to ogle other men. Anytime Kaitlyn tried to lure Cassie close to the bar to order drinks, she'd get flustered and flag down another server.

Nope, she had no guilt leaving Cassie in the large, strong hands of the mysterious bartender.

Then they showed up together this morning to rescue her sorry ass out of the gravel pit. If she hadn't been so freaked out by the shit in her head and the bodies in the warehouse, she would've whooped and chest bumped both of them.

Aaaaand, that thought brought her back to the locker room and the borrowed sweats she was sitting in. The sweats must've been from one of the guys. She was tall, muscular but slender, and they hung on her. Did they even have any women out here? And where was here?

A knock on the door startled her out of her thoughts.

"Are you decent, Miss Savoy?" Master Bellamy asked through the door.

"Uh, yeah. Come on in." The nerves constricted in her belly, not knowing what was going to happen next. Nothing the men had done, except for when they scared the fuck out of her appearing almost from thin air and she turned furry again, had given her any indication they meant harm. That made her just as nervous as waking up and hearing that she had to be put down.

In Kaitlyn's experience, life was about bargaining. There was nothing given for free. If they wanted to help her, then what would she have to do for them in return?

Master Bellamy walked in. He was a handsome man, older than the others, and it was obvious he was in a leadership position from the way Bennett referred to him. The master conveyed an air of quiet confidence in the way he carried his body; he reminded Kaitlyn of all her dojo masters. They had years of training and experience, years of teaching inexperienced kids and adults who thought they knew better only to be proved wrong, and they had no need to show off their abilities. No one would mess with them, and if any idiot wanted to try, it was their wasted energy.

"How are you feeling, Miss Savoy?" he asked.

"Please, call me Kaitlyn. I feel fine. For now. Just a lot of questions."

"I can imagine. We have a lot of questions for you, because Miss Savoy—Kaitlyn—we've never encountered one such as you."

Kaitlyn gave a nervous chuckle, "I'm sure you haven't."

"Not in the way you think. We're like you, the men you've met today: Commander Fitzsimmons, Bennett, Mercury, and myself. Even Jace. Kaitlyn, in my world you are normal. No, what we haven't encountered is a full-grown adult who seems to not know she can shift into a wolf."

Kaitlyn blew out a breath and shrugged. Master Bellamy was sympathetic, his green eyes filled with concern.

"Did you really not know you were a shifter?"

"Nope," she replied. They sat in silence and Kaitlyn shifted in her chair. What did he expect her to say?

"Did your parents ever explain to you what you were?" he finally asked.

Kaitlyn snorted, "Um, no. The whole murder/suicide when I was eleven ended all that. Before my mom died, when she wasn't recovering from my dad's beatings, she was pretty intoxicated. I was always out of the house, for whatever reason I could find. After that, I lived with my aunt and uncle, and they never said anything about four legs or fur. They didn't even own pets."

"I'm sorry, Kaitlyn." She was sick of his sincerity. The pitying looks everyone gave her when they heard her history. Then came the nod of understanding, as if they just put together why she was such a problem child.

"One more question, if you will?" He sensed her growing unwillingness to continue this line of discussion. "Can you recall any sort of physical transformation happening at the time you were going through puberty?"

The blood drained from her face as she began to wring her hands together, those pictures and screams streaming through her mind. "I don't... I don't remember anything about that night."

"That night?"

Her foot tapped the floor and her breathing quickened. Her hands turned white from the force of her grip on herself. Her vision blurred at the edges, going black like she wanted to pass out.

"Kaitlyn? Kaitlyn!"

Her head snapped over to look at him. He was her anchor to consciousness.

"Let's move on to the other reason you're here."

She nodded numbly.

"You're here for answers, but clearly you're not quite ready to go down that road. We'd like you here to train you. To join our team."

Puzzled, she questioned, "Team?"

"We're the law enforcement for our species. We'll explain to you our world, our history, and more specifically what the Guardians do."

"And you're a Guardian?"

"Yes, and you are, too. Look, Kaitlyn, Mercury and Bennett told me about your night together," he paused.

"And what did they tell you?" she asked tersely.

"They sensed you were one of us, which isn't easy with you. It's more obvious, we just know our kind, but you'd been in the club before and they only sensed you as human. But the night you all were together, that changed. And the fact that you could keep up with them suggests you are more like us than other shifters."

She wanted to yell, "Fuck off, old man!" storm away and die of embarrassment. But the curiosity of where he was going with this subject made her keep her ass planted and she forced herself to look him squarely in the face as he talked. She was a grown woman and what she decided to do with her body was her business.

"You see, Kaitlyn, we have two types of Guardians. We have 'normal' shifters because our population is growing and spreading out as technology advances, and we can hide in plain sight easier. But historically, some shifters are born to be Guardians. They are more aggressive, more powerful, have intense protective instincts for those they're in charge of."

"And what does my sex life have to do with the Guardians?"

"Guardians don't mate as easily as others of our kind. We don't know if it's to keep us on edge physically since our mating pool is low, or if it's the nature of the job that we don't come across our mates as readily. With no mate to mellow out our aggressive nature, we need to expend that energy every so often, especially during a full moon. We fight often enough, working out is part of our everyday life, so that leaves…"

"Shopping 'til you drop?" she asked dryly.

Master Bellamy chuckled. "Some Guardians fare better than others. Some turn wolf and run all night in the woods. Some have demons chasing them so hard, it's easier to fuck themselves into oblivion.

"Anyway, we started checking on you. You have black belts in at least three different martial arts and your previous employment shows that you are drawn to security and protection services."

That was a nice way of saying, "you can't hold a job, you irresponsible little girl." Her only steady income was assisting her tae kwon do, judo, and Krav Maga gyms. She was past her first-degree black belt in each one and working her way up Muay Thai.

"So you're investigating me thinking I'm the next new Guardian?"

"Exactly."

She turned to stare at the lockers along the wall. Her world had turned completely upside down. Today, she found out she wasn't human, she was suffering from PTSD she hadn't experienced in over a decade, and the truth of it was her life had turned into a hot mess long before today. This world of Guardians and people who turn into wolves promised answers to her past, present, and future.

She turned back to Master Bellamy. "I'm in."

***

"I'll drive," Cassie said abruptly. Satisfied after talking to Kaitlyn when they brought her up to the interrogation room, Cassie just wanted to get back home—to her reality.

Jace glared at Bennett for shutting him out. But Bennett was watching Kaitlyn walk away, a contemplative look on his face. Cassie worried about Kaitlyn around all these alpha males, but Kaitlyn told her she already felt at peace here, an acceptance she hadn't felt in a long time. And relations between Guardians of the same pack were prohibited, except for mates, but Kaitlyn was told she would know if she ever met her mate. She would be in an eternal "just friends" status with all of her partners out here. Kaitlyn would be alright without Cassie.

"I'll drop you off at the club, Jace."

"Don't you want to learn more?" he asked. "We can talk."

Of course she wanted to learn more. She wanted to do a lot more with Jace, and none of it was talking. If she went back home, with him, she'd learn nothing. They'd be right back where they started last night, with her being putty in his hands. And enjoying it. A lot.

Could she trust him and be like, "Hands to yourself, right?" Or was he too smart and would know that a good way to get her to listen to anything he had to say would be to stay in her condo, completely naked, giving her orgasm after orgasm.

Not willing to chance it, she held her hand out. "I need a little time… to process everything."

He reluctantly, slowly, handed her the keys, as if he'd scare her otherwise. They headed down the stairs to the front door.

Cassie felt both better and worse with Jace next to her. His scent surrounded her, his warmth working its way across her skin. If her pitiful self-defense skills were an issue, he'd take on anything and anyone for her. But, he was still another species and an ex-con.

She'd check on his story. She should ask him to shift for her, too, and validate that, but didn't know if she had it in her to watch it again. Then her mind wouldn't be able to convince herself this was a hallucination and Jace had just slipped her something in her drinks.

Bennett went ahead of them and opened the front door of the lodge. Cassie was ready to step outside, but Jace suddenly yanked her back and whipped her around. *What the—?*

Thunk! A crossbow arrow stuck out of the door where her face would've been.

"Shit," Bennett hissed, slamming the door shut.

"Get down," Jace ordered. She slid down against the wall, with him hovering over her protectively.

Bennett radioed in to the commander and Mercury. Another man, perhaps a wolf, came rushing down the stairs, guns drawn. Like the others, he was tall and ruggedly handsome in his black gear.

"You staying with them?" he asked Bennett.

Bennett nodded, peering out of the window to get a visual on any danger. "Commander and Mercury are close, they'll take the woods."

"Twins?"

Bennett shook his head. "In town on a case."

"I'll take the back." The long-haired shifter disappeared into the depths of the building.

"Jace, those men Kaitlyn killed were Sigma. They're either really stupid or want Kaitlyn bad enough to attack us in our domain."

"Or they're testing us." She felt Jace's reply more than heard it as he covered her protectively with his body, her face pressed into the hard planes of his chest. Reluctant to move from his warmth and scent, she peeked under his arm around his side, to see if she could see anything.

"That's the stupid part. They know they'll die sending anything short of an army up here." Bennett prowled low, getting a look out of the windows.

How did Bennett not expect to get attacked out here? It's a giant, gorgeous, facility in the middle of nowhere, with seemingly open doors and lots of windows. Any backpackers would think they could freeload for a night. Any enemies would see an easy target.

A loud thud on the window made Cassie jump; Jace held her tighter. It sounded like when a robin would hit her big sliding glass doors until she decorated them to keep little feathered broken necks off her deck. Her eyes widened when she saw the deep grooves spider webbing through the glass panes of the window Bennett had just peeked out of. Another cross bolt or a bullet? The window should be shattered. This lodge was turning out to be more than it appeared.

"There's a closet under the stairs, get her in it while Mason and I eliminate the threat from outside." Bennett's eyes glowed like a night predator's, and, sweet mother of all things sane, were those fangs? She drew back from Jace's chest and glanced up. She could see his eyes glittered, even in the light. With his jaw set, she couldn't determine whether he was sporting unusually sharp canines. Could they grow on command?

Jace grabbed her by the shoulders, locking his iridescent blues to her warm browns. "We're gonna make our move. He pointed to her left of the grand staircase, "There should be a closet door. I want you to run as low as you can. I'll cover you." Her eyes darted from his to the stairs. Another thud on the window. Stifling a yelp, she nodded.

Almost on all fours, she scrambled across the room to the stairs. Doing exactly as he said, he stuck to her like glue.

A blast of noise and a rush of heat and wind annihilated the front door, pushed her to the ground. Jace fell on top of her, knocking the breath from her lungs, but just as quickly rolled to the side with his back shielding her from the flying, splintering wood.

A heartbeat of stunned silence was followed by footsteps from outside that were closing in.

"Move!" Bennett yelled. Jace sprung up, taking Cassie with him.

Half-pushing, half-carrying her, they made their way to the stairs.

One gunshot, followed by a quick second and third, then a heavy body hitting the floor. Cassie's heart raced, praying it wasn't Bennett, knowing instinctively he was on Team Good Guys. They reached the door and both dove for the handle when sounds of snarling reached her ears.

Jace pushed her inside with a quick, "Lock it and block it once you get in." Then he spun around to face their enemy. She pulled back, almost shutting the door, but unwilling to cut herself off from what was happening. There were no locks she could feel on her side, and even if there was something to block it with, it was pitch black. Soft fabric brushed against her back, and with one hand holding the door open just a sliver, the other hand frantically searched around to determine what the hell was in here and what could she use to defend herself.

The searching hand went still, along with her breath, when Jace stripped off his shirt, his broad chest sprouting fur. He stepped out of his boots and dropped his pants. Even in the melee, her eyes drifted down to his naked, taut form. He crouched, fur covering him head to toe, taking the form of a goliath, black wolf. A silent intake of air filled her lungs. Jace looked back at her, his teeth bared while his crystalline eyes were still Jace's, imploring her not to panic. Not knowing why, she gave a small nod, and he turned back to face the intruders.

Bennett, as a human, had dropped the first one through the door, but the group pouring in was too big for him to take alone. He was fighting off two more as a wolf, while two more young men rushed around him to charge Jace. One had a gun out and taking aim when Jace pounced.

Moving faster than naturally possible, he took both men down at once. Metal clamored and skittered against the ground. Jace grabbed the closest one by the throat. From the closet, Cassie heard the sickening crunch of bones.

"Jace!"

The second man reared up to grab Jace around the neck and pull him off the fallen one. The glint of a knife flashed, she cried out again, but Jace twisted his body, throwing the offender off and opening him up to Jace's attack.

The door was ripped open out of Cassie's hand, and she found herself face to face with a leering young man who barely looked old enough to drink. He grinned maliciously and grabbed for her neck with a gloved hand.

Reacting without thought, except to be grateful yet again that Kaitlyn was her bestie, Cassie used her forearm to fling his hand away, simultaneously lunging to knee him in the groin. When he roared and hunched over to protect himself, grabbing for her, she rabbit-punched him in the throat and he fell to the ground.

Cassie won that round with surprise on her side. She kicked him in the stomach and jumped over him. Frantically trying to decide which way to go, not wanting to run blindly into more intruders, she searched for Jace. The large, black wolf wrestled with the second man, his mouth around the man's neck. She steeled herself for bone crushing sounds, but Jace held on until the man's struggles ceased.

Bennett was doing the same with his prey. Relieved they weren't mindless killers when wearing fur, she scanned the room, needing to get away from the kid rolling around moaning on the floor. Spotting a gun dropped during the fight, she rushed to grab it. Out of the corner of her eye, a flash of red went snarling by.

Cassie slid to grab the gun and spun around bringing it up in front of her, praying to God it had no safety, it was loaded, and if she pulled the trigger something would go boom.

She lowered the weapon realizing the flash of red had taken out the kid. In her dive for the gun, he had pulled his own weapon and was about to shoot her, but Kaitlyn reached him first.

Suddenly still and quiet, except for Cassie's ragged breaths, the wolves were scrutinizing their environment, sniffing the air. The moment was broken when the man who ran down earlier skidded into the room, completely in the buff.

"How the fuck did they find us? And when the fuck did they get RPGs?" he demanded to no one in particular.

Bennett was the first to turn back to his human form, transitioning seamlessly into his nude human self. Kicking limbs from the fallen out of the way with his bare foot, he made his way to his pile of clothes and bent to dig through his gear. Cassie looked away, subtly clearing her throat.

Flashing a wicked grin her way, quickly replacing it with a dead serious look, he stood holding the same weapon he'd held on Kaitlyn earlier that morning. Was it just this morning they'd gone to retrieve her friend, planning to head right back home? Longest. Day. Ever.

"We'll tranq the ones still alive, throw 'em in the cells." He stretched his arm out to one still form and pulled the trigger. A small metal rod, the tranquilizer, now stuck out from the fallen man's thigh. "Burn the dead."

As Bennett dressed, Jace stretched and rolled his shoulders, back in his glorious human male body. The sunlight filtered in through the obliterated entrance, highlighting his dips and valleys. He really was an impressive specimen, tanned skin covering solid muscle. Jace's tattoo ran from his neck and wrapped around his right shoulder, looking like black waves of water caressing over him. In the light, the scars his tattoos covered were more distinct. He retracted his claws back into fingers, the last change that made him appear truly human, he turned to her.

She swallowed hard. Blood that once coated his fur, now coated his face and chest. His hands were not as bloody as the fangs that had been his primary weapon. He scrubbed his face, realizing what he must look like and went to his own pile of clothes to dress.

A muffled *oomph* made Cassie turn toward Kaitlyn, who now lay prone next to the young intruder she took down. As before, when she transitioned back to a woman, she passed out cold. Cassie rushed to her side, along with the unknown Guardian... who was still naked.

She gently shook Kaitlyn's shoulders, trying to ignore the bare male squatting next to her. *Was someone growling?*

Bennett finished tranqing the two survivors and looked from Jace to the man next to her. "Mason, go get dressed."

Mason scowled at Bennett, then at Jace, who'd finished dressing and was stalking toward him, and stood. "It's not like you have to worry, Miller. You marked the shit outta her. And if I'm not mistaken, she marked you, too. So we can all parade around here naked. No big."

"Marked me?" Cassie asked, glancing between the men.

"Aww, hell," muttered Bennett.

Mason's eyebrows shot up, then a slow grin spread across his face. "Darlin'," he drawled, "you can bite any man you want during sex, ain't nothin' but fun. But bite a wolfman during sex and you're staking your claim, tellin' everyone he's aaalll yours."

Cassie felt the blood drain from her face, then flood right back, as the events from last night, or rather early this morning, filtered through her mind. He did bite her! *Oh God!* She bit him, too!

Jace looked like he wanted to throttle that shit-eating grin off Mason's face. His shoulders back, his fists balled, it was clear he vacillated between taking Mason down and not scaring Cassie. In line with the patience and deliberation he'd shown with her so far, he held back like she knew he would, eyes glowing bright, drilling into Mason's bare back as he exited the room, chuckling.

Master Bellamy kneeled next to her; she never heard his approach. His concerned gaze was on Kaitlyn. "Out cold again, hmmm? Let me take her to my office, we'll check her vitals before we start getting her settled."

Cassie agreed. "I'll go with."

"My apologies, Dr. Stockwell, but you're the wrong kind of doctor. I'll check her over, then we need to get her settled before we can start with her training and find the cause of the blackouts. She won't settle in if she feels the need to watch over you."

"I'll leave when I know she's okay," Cassie said forcefully.

Master Bellamy pinned her with a glare that told her he was unused to his orders being challenged. Well, too bad.

"You would know if she wasn't okay. You two are close, yes?" When she nodded he continued, "You've been her only pack member for years. You two are attuned to each other and you would know if she was in trouble, just like she knew you were in trouble a few minutes ago. Right now, she needs to get cleaned up, again, and you need to get home safely."

Wanting to continue arguing to get her way and stay with her friend, Cassie had to admit he was right. She knew Kaitlyn was in good hands. She also knew she didn't want to find herself facing Jace, talking about marking, and stepping around dead bodies.

With a sigh she stood up, avoided Jace, and looked around at the corpses. What a waste of life. Gone in an instant. And why?

"My God, they're just boys. What happened?"

Mason came strolling back into the room wearing a black long-sleeved top, dark tech pants, combat boots, and head to toe weapons. How do they strip so fast to turn canine?

"She likes 'em young and demented," Mason said, bending to pick up the survivor Bennett left. He gestured with his chin to Jace. "They're usually pretty fucked up kids, lookin' for a reason to kill. They almost find her. But no worries, they're usually over eighteen. Otherwise it gets too messy with families and authorities looking for 'em."

"They almost find who?"

"Madame G," Bennett said grimly. "She's the vampire who heads up the Sigma network in Freemont across the river. Sigma's mission is to kill shifters, but hers is even more demented. She's in charge of all the shifter killings, kidnappings, and most recently, experiments."

"She's a crazy, fuckin' bitch," Mason agreed.

"So who are these guys?" Cassie asked.

"Recruits, probably. Agents are fully trained and her 'program'," Bennett made air quotes, "is a sadistic hell. Recruits are lackeys, expendable, and only the best make it to Agent status. If Madame G wants to cause trouble, make a distraction, or just fuck with us, she sends recruits. Jace, help me get the dead to the pyre."

"Why burn them?" Cassie couldn't help her curiosity. It was morbid standing over the dead, chatting about them. But if it was true these men signed up with malicious intent, well, shit happened and she wanted answers.

As Jace and Bennett each grabbed a guy to haul outside, Cassie tiptoed around the blood, unwilling to be left behind with the bodies.

"Sometimes," Bennett grunted, shifting his burden on his shoulders, "they come back."

"What?"

"Madame G's enhancements," Jace inserted, "they aren't always human when she's done. The bodies could be tracked, they may not be as dead as they should be, or they may be dead, but…" he trailed off.

"How is that possible?"

"We don't know yet. Sigma's been able to dip their fingers in modern technology more than we have, trying to recover from the extinction and fend off their attacks while keeping our people safe."

"What extinction?" Cassie persisted, hurrying to keep up. The two big men moved quickly and efficiently, even with their loads.

Taking sure-footed, heavy steps around the side of the lodge, Jace filled her in. "A few hundred years ago, the network succeeded in wiping out much of our race. We can live for centuries, but you won't find many over two or three hundred years old. The ancients, the oldest of our kind, pure-bloods thought to descend from the original pack, were decimated."

Bennett snorted. "Or at least not heard from again."

They reached what looked like a giant fire pit, and Bennett dumped his body, gesturing to Jace to do the same. Cassie watched in morbid fascination as he deftly lifted the body up off his shoulders and tossed it in.

He brushed off his hands, or at least tried to now that they were even bloodier than before. "Since then, most shifters now all have human blood. So when we shift, we look more like the beast inside of us—a wolf—versus the traditional depiction of a werewolf, which is more of how an ancient would've appeared after transition."

They started back toward the lodge and he kept his hands out of sight for her. Except it still stained his face. She tried not to stare. Not to disturb him, but keep her from mortifying herself that she wanted to swoon seeing this man covered in the blood of someone who would've killed her. Or worse. The bit of fang poking out when Mason was haranguing her had made her pulse quicken. That was mortifying enough.

Bennett continued the explanation, more to stem any awkward silence. "Since then, we've concentrated on concealment and safety. But modern advances have moved so fast in the last century, hell, the last thirty years, so many of our kind have become immersed in the human world and we're struggling to keep up, keep our secret, remain undetected by humans and Sigma. They've been learning and gaining their own technology for use against us. There's only so many shifters, even fewer Guardians, while there seems to be an unlimited supply of minions for Sigma to recruit."

Nearing the front of the lodge again, Commander Fitzsimmons and Mercury were appraising the damage while Mason spoke to them from inside. "...checked the videos, they must've been cloaked. I saw no movement until they held the crossbow up. We'll need to amp up our sensors and widen their zone."

"And fucking steel reinforce all our goddamn doors," Mercury said hotly.

The commander nodded and spoke without looking at any of them. "Mercury, Mason, haul the last two recruits and light them. I need to talk to Bennett and our guests."

Cassie wanted to sigh in frustration, but didn't dare around the formidable commander. The air thickened in his presence, put everyone on edge. And dammit, she wanted to interrogate Jace about the whole marking thing and that was a subject she wasn't bringing up around these men again.

Mercury stepped over the threshold to help Mason, while the rest of them moved inside so Bennett could describe the attack. "Were they after Kaitlyn?" he asked when he was done.

Commander Fitzsimmons gave a curt nod, his expression grim. "We can't assume, but that's the most plausible explanation. They studied her, knew her habits enough to get her to the warehouse, but not enough to realize how powerful she is. Best guess, they were after a shifter, but after she took out an Agent and recruit and we showed interest, Madame G wanted her."

"Will Cassie be safe to go home?" Jace asked, and Cassie gave him a grateful glance, but quickly looked away.

"They'd love to get their hands on you both, but as long as you can keep your mating on the downlow, they shouldn't be interested in her. They'd know we wouldn't give up Kaitlyn for a human. No offense," the commander said in her direction. His look said it didn't really matter if she was offended or not, he was stating a fact.

***

Thanks a lot asshole. Jace was pissed at Commander Fitzsimmons. Cassie avoided looking at him. Jace wanted to hug her hard and inspect her head to toe, run his hands up and down her body to make sure she was okay. He'd been out of his mind when she didn't close the door and he couldn't get to her before that recruit had. His pride almost split him open at how she'd handled herself. Dropped the bastard in two seconds. He was also forever in Kaitlyn's debt for jumping in when she had.

No collapsing and sobbing for his mate. She was distracting herself, trying to learn about shifter-kind and what happened. She was also distracting herself from him. He didn't interrupt as Commander Fitzsimmons told her what to keep an eye out for and safety measures to take, he just stood and looked his fill. Her sexy pixie cut was mussed up giving her a sassy look that fit her so well.

He was leaning back to get a quick look at her butt in her capris, to tide him and his raging emotions over, when Bennett leaned over and spoke quietly in his ear, "Second door on the right there's a mud room, in case you want to clean up a little."

Jace brought his hands up from being clasped behind him. Cassie managed to get almost no blood on her and for that he was grateful. He however, was covered with enough for the both of them. Fuck, no wonder she was trying not to look at him. She seemed comfortable enough around Bennett, but Bennett didn't take her home last night.

"Thanks man." He clapped Bennett on the shoulder, murmured to Cassie he'd be right back, and jogged inside.

After a quick rinse off, he was back out by Cassie's side. She still wouldn't look at him.

Look at me, he pleaded silently, cursing the turn of events this morning. When he woke up with her nestled in his arms, he knew she would be his. He'd feed her, they'd hang out, she'd get to know him. Then maybe when the news hit of what he was and what his recent past had been like, he could help her move past it.

Instead, she not only found out he was a murderer and a different species, she got an eyewitness account of both. Could she grow to not only understand him, but accept him? Cassie was his fated mate. It was unusual to find one's fated mate in the first fifty years of life. They lived too long, needed to learn how long and lonely their life could be, and why a mate should be treasured above all else. They needed to learn to protect their mate and any offspring against the perils of Mother Nature, human nature, and the rest of nature that wanted to kill all of their kind. If Cassie rejected him, it would indeed be a long, lonely life.

Look at me. Cassie stood with her back to him, arms stubbornly crossed in front of her chest, nodding at Commander Fitzsimmons' instructions. She was astute; she knew he was assessing her ability to keep quiet about everything she learned today, otherwise the Guardians would have to deal with the situation. They didn't hurt innocents, even if it was for the greater good, but they could delete her memories of today, alter them in some way.

Jace wasn't sure which of the Guardians had that ability as they differed with each shifter, like his power of persuasion. Human minds could crumple under the invasion, especially if the wielder didn't have absolute control over their gift. Cassie was strong, mentally nimble, she wouldn't crumble, but the protective male in him would not let these men infringe on her, or invade her, in any way.

Look at me. He made the decision a long time ago that he would never use his abilities on the person who would become his partner in life, no matter the reason. Cassie being human, made him even more determined in his resolution. A breach of trust of that magnitude would erode the foundation of matehood. Soon the one who is the most important to you in your ever-long life would wonder if they were persuaded to give up an argument, agree with a new car purchase, even change their mind about the toilet seat being left up.

Finally, she turned to face him. Cleaned of blood now, he remained still as her gaze flicked quickly up and down his length. Repressing a self-satisfied smirk when he saw a flash of heat in her eyes, all he asked was, "You ready?"

He greedily drank her in as she walked toward him, back ramrod straight, hands stiff at her side. Sexy little shrink, trying not to betray her nervousness by running her hands through her hair. No wonder she wore it so short. She would continually fuss with her hair the first half hour she was at the club on any given night. Then as she relaxed, so did her fidgeting... slightly.

"Actually," she cleared her throat, "can you find a ride home? I'd like to drive myself. Alone."

Jace sharply inhaled, inadvertently smelling her divine flower and vanilla scent. He let it glide down into his lungs, easing him. Slowly, he exhaled. "I don't think that's a good idea."

"It doesn't matter what you think," she snapped. In a softer tone, "I appreciate your concern, Jace. I really do. This is a lot to take in. You, them, the attack..." Her gaze drifted to someplace far away. She shook it off. "I need time to think."

"You could still be in danger, Cassie. I can't just let you leave on your own. Are the Guardians okay with this?" He looked up, searching for some support. Mason had disappeared inside to help Commander Fitzsimmons with clean-up efforts. Mercury was avidly watching their interplay from the landing while Bennett was discreetly trying to drag him inside. Mercury flung off his arm and stalked in. Bennett shot Jace a brief *you poor bastard* nod before leaving. So they were okay with letting her view their world, their home, and allowing her to go?

"Their main concern is Kaitlyn. I think there's something pretty significant to them about her. I'm getting in the way. Trying to protect me, but keep their secrets from me, is inconvenient."

Fucking Guardians. As Jace's mate, Cassie was his problem and they wanted her to be his problem somewhere else. They assessed her, she wasn't breaking under shock, felt she wasn't a threat to their existence, so back to business as usual. So it was, "hey thanks for lending a fang, but it's time for you and your pesky human to go."

Keeping his restraint, determined not to scare her off any more than he had the last few hours, he kept his tone even, "You're my main concern Cassie. I'd like to see you home safely. What if they're still out there?" He gestured toward the woods.

"Commander Fitzsimmons assured me they aren't. I have his number programmed into my phone, just in case. I need time, Jace." Warm brown eyes sought out his. "I just want to go home."

Losing himself in their depths, he waged an internal battle. Protective mate or considerate prospective boyfriend? Fucking Guardians! The more he pushed, the more distance she would keep between them. If he got his way, resentment would build within her. He didn't know her past, but he sensed she was strongly independent, probably learned to rely on herself at an early age.

Considerate prospective boyfriend it was. "Will you call me when you get home?"

Relief flashed across her face. He recited his number. She punched his digits into her phone, grabbed her keys, and headed to her car. He beat her there, holding the door open for her, feeling helpless otherwise. Wishing he could go in for a kiss, but knowing she wasn't in the right place mentally for it, he waited while she climbed in.

When she didn't say anything, just started the engine, he let the door fall shut. This wasn't going at all like he planned.

Before rolling off, she surprised him by opening the window. "They'll get you home right?"

There was no way in hell he was strolling up to any of the guys here and asking for a ride. The commander probably wouldn't even look at him or acknowledge the request. Mercury and Bennett would double over in laughter. At least Bennett would. Mercury, a little clueless about the human emotion part of his nature, would give him that quizzical look Jace came to associate with him and then follow Bennett in peals of laughter. Mason was an asshole and barely tolerated by his own pack, the Guardians. No, he would get back to his loft above Pale Moonlight the old-fashioned way. It was a long haul, but he needed a four-legged run through the woods to think after a day like today.

"Yeah, don't worry about me. I'll hang out here 'til I hear from you." Could a mature alpha male get the warm fuzzies? She'd stopped to ask about him, she was worried. There was hope yet.

Cassie passed him a hesitant smile as she raised her window and drove off.

Jace watched her go, his heart at the pit of his stomach. Commander Fitzsimmons said he and Mercury had combed through the woods between the quarry and here. They saw no signs of Sigma, other than the trail the group of rookies left. He'd trust their senses that told them all were taken care of. The two survivors would be questioned heavily.

Jace headed back to the lodge. Commander Fitzsimmons was discussing surveillance and detection, and renovations with Mason. The other two Guardians were on clean-up duty.

"Mr. Miller," came the commander's stern voice, "if you're planning to stay, grab a mop."

"Dude, she left you?" Mercury was completely confused.

Jace only heard rumors of the shifter's past and what he'd seen of the Guardian's interactions only strengthened his belief in them. The male was almost completely inept around humans and that included shifters in human mode. The intricacies of emotion, especially the interplay between males and females were a complex knot Mercury had yet to undo. He avoided women, except when he was wound up and then Bennett ran the interactions, picking out the willing participants and then seeing them out when everything was finished. Mercury rarely came in for just a drink. Women were too drawn to him, his size and unique looks went a long way. Until he opened his mouth. His brutal honestly and oblivious directness earned him more than a few cheek slaps.

"Yeah, she needs some time." Jace saw it still didn't register with Mercury. In the other male's mind, Cassie was Jace's mate. Why wouldn't she stay by his side?

Bennett slapped him on the back and handed him the mop. "Don't worry, Jace. She didn't run screaming at any point today. That's something." The sympathy emanating from Bennett made Jace want to turn wolf, grab his shit and go. Hell, he'd just leave his clothes and run naked from the edge of town to the club. But Bennett was right and if anyone knew the inner turmoil Jace was in, it was Bennett.

"Why break it gently, right? Just lay it all out there." Jace said drily. Bennett chuckled, Mercury nodded matter-of-factly, the commander ignored him.

"You shoulda just told her that's the way it was. Worked your magic on her," Mason said arrogantly. "I mean if you gotta have a human mate, why not?"

A low growl strained to rumble out of Jace's chest, but a perceived threat in the Guardian headquarters would not go over well. Jace hadn't worked on his self-control for the last twelve years to lose his shit over this asshole, esteemed Guardian or not.

Bennett stiffened, ready to jump in if Jace turned on Mason. Mercury watched Jace for an answer, no doubt wondering why Jace wouldn't use his gift if he had one. Why not save himself the long walk back to town and just tell Cassie how it was? Commander Fitzsimmons was looking over his shoulder, evaluating Jace's reaction.

"Because," Jace spoke evenly, "I will never falsely persuade my mate no matter what."

Mason's mouth curled up in a smug smirk. "Meanwhile, she's got you by the short hairs. Enjoy your run."

Asshole. Jace continued mopping while Mason walked out.

"Soooo," Bennett said, rubbing the back of his neck. "You hungry Jace? Blood and guts always gets my appetite going. We'll break to eat before we fix the door."

"Yeah, but which twin is cooking tonight?" Mercury asked. Malcolm and Harrison were the twin shifters; tall, dark, and deadly. They were always together—on their ops and with their women. "You don't wanna stay if it's Malcolm. He's a shit cook."

Jace's mouth twitched up at Mercury's bluntness. They must run this place like firefighters with twenty-four hour, round-the-clock shifts where everyone rotates cooking and cleaning.

"It's Malcolm," Commander Fitzsimmons informed them. "But he's bringing home burgers from The Steak Shack. I told him to bring extra so you might as well stay."

Chapter Seven

Cassie whipped into her parking spot at the mental health center. Running late, she grabbed her purse and practically bolted through the employee entrance at the back of the clinic. She never woke up late and was always on time. Since she was still building her patient base, her mornings weren't often booked solid. Today, of course, she had a last minute booking in the first slot of the day. Normally, when she knew no patients were scheduled at the beginning of the day, she meandered in right at nine a.m. and spent the first hour reading ahead on upcoming cases for the day.

Today started shitty, and was looking to stay that way. Her alarm didn't go off so she woke up to the admin assistant calling her to ask if it was okay to schedule a patient right away. He was a new patient, had requested her, and was there waiting. Patients equaled money. She shot out of bed and ran through the shower, grabbed a granola bar, and bolted out the door.

Now as she rushed down the hall to her office, she grimaced. She literally ran into someone during her run yesterday and had the road rash to prove it on her knee. And no wonder Cassie had been the one to hit the ground. The woman had been tall, well built, and absolutely stunning. Her bright green eyes shone with good humor as she helped Cassie up. Her dark, almost black, hair was as memorable as her athletic body, encased in bright performance gear. The sides of her hair were an inch long, if that, and the longer hair on top was done up in a fashionable faux hawk. She had apologized profusely to Cassie, claiming to have been checking out another jogger in the park. Scraped up, Cassie brushed it off, not wanting to call any more attention to herself than the fall had. The woman had introduced herself as Alex and ran alongside Cassie after she shook off the knee pain and resumed along her path. They chatted companionably and it was the highlight of Cassie's week.

It had been a long, lonely week with more major blows to the ego and it was only Wednesday. When Cassie first got home after leaving Jace in her rearview mirror, she had wandered aimlessly around her condo, wanting to change her bedding, but changing her mind because she didn't want to lose Jace's scent and wash away the memories of their time together. Not that she had to worry, the whole condo was full of reminders of him: the entryway where they first came together, the stove where he'd made her breakfast, the table where they'd sat together. She couldn't concentrate, didn't yet want to face the new world Jace showed her and how she felt about it all. With Kaitlyn living and training with the Guardians, she had no one to sit on the couch with her to drink wine, eat ice cream, and add to the evidence that men suck.

Sunday, she had woken up determined to live her life as close to pre-Jace as she could. That afternoon, she called a good friend to see if an afternoon of shopping would drag her spirits out of the gutter. The memory of the conversation made her wince more than any knee scrape ever could.

She summoned false enthusiasm when her friend answered.

"Hey Emma! I was wondering if you wanted to meet me over in Freemont for a little retail therapy?"

Awkward silence.

"Oh, Cassie... Oh, I can't make it, sorry ..."

Then Cassie heard a man's familiar voice on the other end call, "I'm throwing some coffee on, Em. What kind do you want?"

"Holy. Shit," Cassie said, shocked.

"I'm sorry, Cassie. It just happened. I just came over to see if he was okay and—"

"Emma? What kind of java, baby?" Grant continued on the other end oblivious to either the phone call or who was on the other end, or both.

Emma went silent, probably to point to the phone mouthing Cassie's name.

"So Emma, tell me. Was I not home when you went on your 'my condolences tour?' Or has this been going on for awhile?" Cassie asked angrily. She and Grant had double-dated with Emma and

her beau-of-the-month several times. Cassie thought maybe Grant would get tired of awkwardly chatting with Emma's new plus one every time, but he never complained. Now she knew why.

"No, of course not. It just happened," Emma pleaded.

"Just happened? Really? He's been single less than two days. How'd you even find out?"

"Grant called Ryan yesterday, who told Jess, who called me. I just wanted to see if he was okay. I knew you'd be all right, Cassie," Emma finished, lamely.

"Right, that's it. I'd totally be fine." Cassie took a deep breath, remembered exactly who she had went home with two nights ago and realized she was being a hypocrite. Except Jace was a complete stranger, not an old pal of Grant's. "And you're right. I am fine. Hope it works out for you two." She cut the call off.

The rest of Sunday, Cassie went for a run, ate more Ben & Jerry's, aimlessly wandered the mall, picked up some froyo to take home, and went to bed. The first part of the week was work, running, and more ice cream. Meeting Alex, aside from getting plastered on the running path, had been the highlight of her week.

Cassie maneuvered through the hallways to her office and was met by Amy from the front desk.

"Dr. Stockwell! Good, you're here." She spoke rapidly as Cassie unlocked her office and headed in.

"Can I just bring him back for you since he's been waiting a few minutes?"

Amy's eyes sparkled and she was almost dancing in place.

"Sure, Amy."

"He's—he's so— he's just—" Her eyes glazed and she sighed. "I'll go get him." And she rushed off.

With only a few minutes to spare, she hung up her sweater and logged into her computer, hoping to bring up the patient's file and read his name before he arrived. She was curious to find out who had flustered Amy so.

She heard them approach and Amy breathlessly told him he could head in and shut the door behind him. Cassie swiveled around, not wanting her back to a new patient. Her stomach dropped when she saw who walked in.

"Hey, Cassie," Bennett said, after he shut the door. "I mean, Dr. Stockwell, now that I'm your patient."

"What are you doing here? Is Jace okay?" she asked, growing alarmed.

"No, he's fine. But just my two cents, Doc, don't keep him waiting too long. We might have more time to wander this planet, but you can't get back lost time and you never know when it runs out." Solemn lines and his pensive expression indicated he'd been in such a lonely limbo. He took a seat in one of the plush chairs across from her. He wore jeans and a pullover today. How many knives did he have strapped under his sweater?

"Okay." Still perplexed, Cassie asked, "So what are you doing here?"

"I'm here as a patient." He ran a hand through his blond locks, which stayed arranged as if ready for a photo shoot. "You were right, you know. About how I'm barely holding it together. I don't know how much longer I can hang on. I didn't know who could help me before, but here you are. A shrink and you know about us."

Cassie considered what he said. She'd only meant to throw him off that day in the interrogation room, to mess with him like he'd been trying to do to her. But her instincts had been spot on. A firm believer that most people could use professional guidance, she supposed that belief now extended to shifters.

"Here's the deal, Bennett. What you say here," she waved her hand between them, "completely confidential. I'll treat you like a normal patient. The only difference will be my notes. I'll leave out the whole 'werewolf' bit."

"Do you have to take notes at all?"

"Yes, they help me remember what we talked about so I can outline the best way to help you. I'll keep them as human appearing as possible." They were supposed to remain confidential but nothing was safe these days. If they did get out, she didn't want anyone to see the phrases "turns into a wolf" or "shapeshifts" and come after her with a straight jacket.

"Well, all right then," Bennett said and reclined back. "Where do we start?"

***

Their hour wrapped up quickly. Cassie scribbled ferociously, pausing only to assess whether or not to include something. She learned much about Guardians and much about the shifters themselves. She'd reflect on that later. With wine.

"I guess, Doc." Bennett stood. "I'd better be going." Just like that, he was back to being the competent second-in-command of the West Creek Guardians. Not the haggard, worn looking man who'd experienced horrible personal tragedy, witnessed trauma as a normal part of his job, and managed to bottle it all up inside so he could face another day.

Cassie got up to let him out of her office, musing about how she might solidly build a bigger patient base as the confidant of a race of creatures everyone thought was for fairy tales. The things Bennett would be talking about with her at his weekly sessions would sound like they came out of someone's imagination. Stories she'd have someone committed for …

Oh. Shit.

"Bennett…" Cassie said, closing her door again. "Are vampires real, too?"

Bennett's deep blues took on a guarded expression. After a moment's hesitation he spoke. "Yes. Why?"

Cassie released her breath, not realizing she'd been holding it. She leaned her head back against the door, dread building.

"I wish I could tell you, but I can't. I'll just say, that I may need to review an old case."

"They're dangerous, Cassie. Not as willing to blend as we are. You aren't our food source like you are for them. Our species are historically at war."

"Sounds like there's a story there."

"There always is, but like you said, we're out of time, Doc. Jace'll tell you everything you want to know."

She wanted to groan. She'd think about Jace over the wine, too. Maybe.

"Remember my story, Doc." He opened the door behind her, forcing her to move out of the way.

"It's just so complicated," she muttered under her breath as he walked away.

"No it's not," he called back, continuing down the hall.

Sighing, Cassie returned to her desk to review her next patient. She had a lot to think about—her new case, Bennett, an old case who was now committed in Freemont General Hospital's psych ward, and Jace. She needed to pick up more wine. And ice cream.

***

It'd been two weeks. Thirteen days, but who's counting? How much time did she need? She was single. They went nuclear together. And he was still waiting for her to talk to him again.

"Amy," he said, leaning over the counter. It was the end of the day, the waiting room was bare and the petite receptionist was already mesmerized by him. He looked her directly in the eyes, forcing her gaze to lock with his ice-blue eyes. "Amy, schedule me as Dr. Stockwell's last patient of the day, in place of the cancellation."

Five minutes earlier, the cancellation had met with the power of Jace's stare in the hallway and immediately decided to skip a week in mental health visits. Jace couldn't force people to do what he wanted, he couldn't control them, but he could strongly persuade them, and it helped if they secretly wanted to do the task requested of them. Cassie's last patient really just wanted to go home and put his feet up after a long day. Just like the receptionist really wanted to please a handsome male.

Amy immediately entered Jace's information into the computer, a flush creeping up her face, her breath coming quicker. This mark was easy.

"Just let me know where her office is, and I'll see myself there."

Amy hesitated.

"Amy," Jace said again, catching her eyes.

She nodded and rattled off directions, holding his stare.

"Thank you," he said. "Now go home, take a nice bath, and forget about work."

She nodded, dazed. He left her as she shut down her computer and grabbed her purse.

He made his way through the maze of hallways, never having been in this building but following Cassie's unique floral and vanilla scent. He'd wanted to kill Bennett over that scent yesterday.

The club had been open, but it was still early and no one was really there. Jace was wrapping up the books when he walked out and caught a whiff of Cassie. And it was coming from Bennett.

Jace hauled Bennett off his stool and pinned him over the bar, his arm across Bennett's neck. There would have been more of a fight, but Jace used the element of surprise and was a pissed-off mate.

"Wha—?" That was all Bennett could get out, his face turning red.

"Why. Do. You. Have. Her. Scent?" His fangs elongated to rip into Bennett's throat as soon as he answered.

"Pa-tient," Bennett spit out.

Not expecting that answer, Jace eased up a bit. "What the fuck's that supposed to mean?"

"I'm her patient."

Jace was confused. Patient? Cassie was a psychologist… Oh. He let the man up off the bar, but held onto his shirt.

"Why do you smell like her?" His anger was starting to gear up again.

"I don't know," Bennett said, throwing Jace's hands off him. "Probably from the candles and shit she has in her office. Smells like a fucking cake, but it's supposed to be calming."

Bennett grabbed his stool, righted it, and sat back down in a huff. Jace stood dumbly, not knowing what to do next. The woman had him strung tighter than ninety-nine cents in a dollar store.

"I put in a good word for you, too, bro. But maybe I should tell her to take her time. Think about it for month." Bennett said, anger in his taunt. "No three months. Maybe your blue balls will teach you a lesson by then."

"Sorry."

"Well, lucky for you I get where you're coming from. Otherwise, I wouldn't need a shrink."

"Look man, I'm sorry." Jace had acted like a dick. He'd heard the rumors about Bennett's past. Of course, he'd understand.

"Well, you should be. Looks like I drink free all night. All weekend."

Relieved, Jace said, "You got it, my man. Let me get you a cold one."

He handed the frosty mug over to Bennett and waited until the man took the first pull. "How's she doing?"

"Fine," Bennett said, wiping his mouth. "Overwhelmed."

"I get that. I get it's all new. I'm new, but she has to feel it."

Bennett lifted one shoulder in a shrug. "We all have shit in our past, fucking up our future. Even humans."

How profound.

It got Jace thinking, though. She'd asked him not to call. Didn't trust having him in her home. But she couldn't turn away a patient.

That thought led him to her office door. He heard her in there, typing away. He didn't sense anyone in the nearby offices. Perfect.

He opened the door and stepped in, closing it behind him. "Dr. Stockwell."

Cassie's heart stopped as she swiveled toward the door. He was here. *Ohmigod.* He was devastating. His woodsy, fresh scent filled her office, overpowering the calming candle scents that were doing nothing for her now. His eyes shined, like he was stalking prey. Today he was wearing a black muscle shirt, black jeans, and his Harley boots. Not much different from when she'd last seen him, but the effect no less enticing.

The set of his jaw determined, he stalked closer. She remained sitting, leaning farther back into her chair, wishing she could disappear into it. For two weeks, she'd done well avoiding thinking about him, at least for ten-minute-long stretches. Her condo was cleaner than it'd ever been. Her living room even had a new paint job. She'd run more than she ever had in her life. That had nothing to do with her massive ice cream and wine consumption.

When he reached her, he squatted down in front of her between her knees, as far they were allowed to spread in her A-line skirt. She tried not to think about what she decided to wear today in her usual attempt to look like a mature, mental health professional, and not a coed. The thigh-high stockings and garters were just because she hated the way pantyhose sagged after a long day.

His eyes briefly closed as he inhaled her scent.

"Cassie," he breathed.

Her heart pounded. She couldn't think straight if he kept doing this, kept making her feel like the most special being, the highlight of his life.

"J. Miller," she said, repeating the file name she was given before he entered her life again.

His mouth cocked up on the side causing her stomach to summersault. Her center was already warming, making her want to squirm in her seat, but afraid of where that would lead her, where it would lead them.

"I needed to see you." His eyes roamed up and down her body, pausing on her exposed garter line, his nostrils flaring.

She tried to sit up straighter, show a little less leg, but it was impossible with him parked in between her thighs. It was impossible when all she really wanted to do was slide down closer and rub against him, ease the burn that was spreading. Ease the ache that had been plaguing her for weeks.

"You could've called," she said.

"You told me not to." He finally raised his gaze to hers, jaw clenched. "I was respecting your wishes."

She didn't know what to say. Didn't know what to tell him. Her doctor's brain said to tell him the truth. Yet what good would it do. His kind wouldn't understand. Her time with Bennett showed her how important mating was to shifters. They became each other's worlds, you didn't know where one person ended and their mate began. That terrified her, on so many levels. That this man, the one she'd been avoiding even looking at for months, could be hers completely. She'd be his even *more* completely. Bonded to his life force. If something happened to him, that was it. She was toast. If nothing happened to him. She was his. For centuries…

"Cassie, give me a chance," he pleaded quietly.

She opened her mouth to say something, but closed it again. She didn't know what to say. She was scared to accept him. Scared she'd have the courage to tell him to go away.

"Cassie." He exhaled her name. His eyelids fell half-mast, he leaned in and captured her mouth.

- 126 -

He took control and she gave it up to him, their tongues twining and dancing around each other. His large, warm hands caressed her thighs, running up and down their length. She wrapped her arms around his shoulders and held on as he moved one hand past her garters, stroking her through her panties.

She almost came instantly, crying out against his mouth.

He gripped her panties and tried to tug them down. The weight of her sitting made it difficult, the garters fueling his desire. He growled, rising to his feet, bringing her with him, their tongues still entwined.

Instead of sliding the panties down, he twisted them off entirely. He caught her surprise with his mouth and raised her skirt up past her bare bottom. His hard length pressed against her belly; she ran her hands down his broad shoulders, down his stomach, and popped open the fastener on his jeans.

Once the zipper came down, his member sprang free into her waiting hand. Holding her to him, he kicked the chair out of the way, and moved her backward, lifting her onto her desk. Supplies fell in a distant clatter, but it didn't matter if it was her computer falling to the floor. Nothing would stop what was going to happen next.

He used his hands to lift her legs around his sides. She guided the steel length of him to her. Without pause, he slid into her slick heat. She sighed into his mouth as he gripped her legs. They were wrapped around him so tightly, his thrusts weren't deep. They rocked together a few times, priming the need raging through them both until he slid his hands to her knees, pushing her legs farther apart so he could pump into her. He leaned over her, licking her tongue with his.

She held onto his shoulders, gladly allowing her body to be dominated by him. There'd been too many long nights of interrupted dreams. Dreams about Jace, so real she could feel him on her skin, smell him on her sheets, woke her up panting, alone, and unrequited. Her body had been waiting for him.

Every thrust was ecstasy. They kept their mouths fused together, muffling their groans and cries until the final stab sent them both over the edge. Cassie screamed into his mouth, clutching him for dear life as the orgasm ripped through her.

They rocked gently together with the aftershocks, their bodies squeezing out every bit of pleasure possible. Cassie buried her head into his neck, breathing hard.

He slid out of her and helped her off her desk. She felt empty without his heat filling her.

Her rational thoughts returned, lining up into something resembling common sense. While someone else may dream of intense office sex, she took her position too seriously to risk termination. She worked damn hard to get here, all on her own... had the student loans to prove it.

"You should go." Cassie gazed at the floor while straightening her skirt.

Jace glanced at her, buttoning his jeans after tucking all his maleness back into place, and sighed. "I came here to talk with you, not…" He gestured toward the desk. "Can we meet later? Tomorrow? Whenever?"

She paused, intending to shoot him down again. This was still too much, too soon.

"It can be in public," Jace interjected. "Like a real date, so you can actually get to know me."

It made sense. She was fiercely attracted to him and for all he said about being mates and her resistance, he'd been extremely patient. She found that while she may not be ready to commit to centuries together as soul mates, the idea of a date sounded nice.

"Okay."

He smiled, a true smile reaching all the way to his eyes, crinkling them at the corners. Heaven help her, her bad boy had a dimple. Between what just happened in her *freaking office* and that smile, she was careening past infatuation to real feelings.

"Great, tomorrow at six. I'll pick you up. Wear something casual." He leaned in, brushed her cheek with his lips.

"Jace, I have commitment issues," she blurted. "All this is bringing them to the forefront. I'm not ready to deal and that's what you've been waiting on."

He caressed her cheek. "You're worth waiting for."

As if he didn't trust himself to not take her on the desk again, he turned abruptly and left. She stepped out to watch him walk away and groaned inwardly. Dr. Ego turned the corner at the other end of the hall, heading her way.

When he saw her, Dr. Ego's nostrils flared, one dark eyebrow raised. Cassie prayed the copious candles in her office masked any scent of sex permeating the hallway. She stood tall, pretending her panties were still on and not laying somewhere on the floor behind her, and faced him, pulling her door a little further shut behind her.

"Dr. Egron." What wouldn't sound paranoid? *You're still here?* No. *What's up?* No, he was a dick, they weren't that friendly. "Working late?"

"Not as late as you it seems, Dr. Stockwell," he replied snidely, as he walked past. "I'm heading out, if you'd arm the system behind you?"

"Sure, I'll finish up my notes and be on my way."

"Dr. Stockwell?" His cultured voice always grated on her nerves. He faced her before he turned into the hallway Jace had gone down. "Do take care, leaving so late. Crime may not be on the rise, but suspicious persons have been seen loitering in the vicinity."

Shocked at his concern, that he could be anything but condescending, she nodded her thanks and he left.

Another warning from an unexpected source. Interesting. When she had gone running yesterday, with the woman she had been knocked down by, as they parted ways Alex called, "Watch yourself, little lady," then grinned and ran off. Maybe she should mention it to Bennett at his next appointment.

She sank back into her office, snapped up her panties off the floor, retrieved all of her desk items, and threw them back on her desk. Then she collapsed into her chair.

Eventually, she was going to have to face her past. And she wasn't talking about the patient she'd had committed for raving about fanged monsters hunting him in the streets and stalking his home. No, even farther back than that, before she came to live with Kaitlyn, and her aunt and uncle. Back to her deceased mother, her grieving schizophrenic father, and their life on the run.

There was a reason she took an interest in mental health. A reason why she thrived on dependability and predictability. A reason why a dependable, predictable Grant suited her as a spouse and she never went beyond overly fond of him. A major reason why an obsession, this all-consuming need for another being, terrified her.

But living without Jace, trying not to think about him these last couple of weeks, wasn't working for her. Neither were their spontaneous sex sessions. Oh, they worked physically. Really well. But they left her in emotional turmoil. Dating him was a good start; get to know her shape-shifting ex-con bartender as just a man.

Chapter Eight

She sighed contentedly, his arm and leg draped over her as they lay together. Warm, cozy, and protected, she snuggled against him, a sleepy smile playing at her lips.

"X! Get up here! We need to talk." A loud voice drilled right into her skull.

Fuck! X sat up immediately awake, shaking off her dream as quickly as possible. Dreams like that were dangerous, made her want things she'd given up long ago. Gave her something even more dangerous—hope.

"Yes, ma'am," X replied, knowing Madame G was still in her head and would hear her. *At least she can't read thoughts.* There didn't seem to be much Madame G couldn't do, but if she could read thoughts, X would've been dead long ago.

X crawled into her standard dress: black, long-sleeved tech-wear shirt and black leather pants tucked into black combat boots. She slung her weapons belt around her waist and finished off sheathing various knives across the rest of her body. She already had some under her clothes, the ones she slept with. Gotta be ready at all times with her life.

X fluffed up her hair and gave it some attitude. It threw people off – the punk chic do. Made their first impression one to not take her seriously. She supplemented that with her candid comments, giving her the element of surprise when she needed to put someone down. Or at least put them in their place, but unfortunately in her life, putting them down was the most common outcome.

She armed her system and walked out of the room. She not only wanted to know if anyone tried to get in or succeeded at getting in, she wanted to know if Madame G ever slummed it down in the bowels of her lair.

X maneuvered though those bowels effortlessly. She could do it blindfolded if she needed to. Had, in fact, to make sure she could. It'd been almost ten years since she was brought here, she made sure she knew as much as possible about her "home." Death targeted the unprepared.

Climbing into the elevator, she was about to hit the button for Level G, named for Madame G's suite level, when the redheaded hooker came running in. Mental eye roll.

"What's up Red?" X asked.

Red adjusted her tits and grinned. "I think G's finally putting me to work."

Another mental eye roll. If Red—*what the fuck was her name again?*—wanted to chance fate and refer to their mistress as just "G" accidently in front of her, it was her funeral—after a slow, painful death. X made sure she *always* referred to their nightmare mistress in respectful terms—even in her head.

And what did she mean finally getting put to work? Red was being used as training material for the new recruits. Training material, as in, on her back while they practiced their seduction techniques on her—rumor had it—very willing body.

X suppressed a shudder, the memory of her seduction training threatened to rise. She shoved it back into the dark depths of her brain with all things bad that had happened in the last decade.

"Going to the field?" X asked.

Red nodded excitedly and bit her lip. "Maybe."

The elevator finally made it up through the five subfloors and the first two above ground levels of the lair to Level G. It opened up into the opulent majesty that was Madame G's main office. If Madame G didn't want someone there, the elevator would've dumped them off at the first two levels. No one got to Madame G if Madame G didn't expect them first.

Plush red leather sofas and chairs sat off to each side of the black walnut monstrosity that was the desk. Madame G claimed red was the color of royalty but X suspected that bloodshed didn't ruin it as quickly as regular brown leather. The floor was polished dark wood, scrubbed by the new recruits weekly. Poor bastards. If polishing was the only thing they were made to do up here they were lucky. Very lucky.

The walls had royal purple fabric hangings spaced between self-portraits of Madame G herself, over the decades. Madame G holding the head of shifter she'd decapitated, with her foot propped up on his prone body. Madame G naked from behind, astride an unknown male, her head half-turned toward the painter, her arm raised, claws extended and ready to strike the male she was atop. Madame G with five new recruits begging like dogs in front of her.

Those new recruits were probably just as willing as X had been the day she was "recruited."

Madame G appeared out of nowhere. Red jumped, X suppressed a snicker. She expected nothing less of her mistress.

Red swooped down into a curtsy while X assumed a proper submissive position, standing with legs slightly apart, hands clasped in front where Madam G could always see them, head bowed.

"X, I'm getting impatient. Where are we at with the mating couple?" Madame G's voice, like her appearance, had the qualities of Asian origin. X seriously doubted Madame G had ever stepped foot overseas, much less lived anywhere in Asia long enough to pick up an accent that stuck for centuries. She was old, but X heard no stories beyond those of Madame G's terror in the States.

She probably played off her looks like X did. Madame G was tall and willowy, with pitch black, long hair kept in a high bun. She always looked down on those before her with those dark almond eyes atop high cheekbones. Her porcelain skin rarely flushed, and when it did, those in the vicinity suffered.

"Mistress, they have begun making contact again. If I have a team at the ready, we can snatch and grab on my call."

Madame G inclined her head. "Very well. Choose your people and make it happen."

She turned to Red, "Janice, I have an assignment that requires your special talents."

Red—Janice—nodded excitedly.

"We need to harvest a shifter's seed. You may need to have sex with one of those vile creatures. And from what we've learned of their disgusting nature, perhaps more than one. Do you think you're strong enough?"

"Of course! Uh, Madame G," Janice threw in to make up for any perceived disrespect. "In the name of the mission," she stated dutifully.

"Very good," Madame G almost purred. "X, you may go. I need to fill young Janice here in on how she can further our cause."

X executed a half-bow and retreated to the elevator only half hearing the plan. She could almost feel Janice's excitement growing. Janice was one of those recruits who actually volunteered for Madame G's mission. They tended to be heavily fucked-up individuals. In Janice's case, she was a paranormal groupie and getting to have sex with vamps on a regular basis was a dream come true.

Sex with shifters would be the stuff of her messed-up fantasies: vigorous, insatiable, and none of that fatiguing bloodletting afterward.

As the door shut, X began planning who and what she would need. And mentally prepare for the look of betrayal from Cassie.

Intel came in that there was activity at The Den. Finally! Janice squirmed in her seat, the heavy bass of the club's music vibrating through her chair making her more stimulated than she already was. Ever since Madame G told her about her assignment, planned out meticulously, they'd cut her off from her normal duties otherwise. She couldn't have the scent of other males on her, much less vamps. Not all recruits were vamps… unfortunately. Janice was tired of human dick. They just didn't have the stamina to satisfy her more evolved tastes.

They were very routine, Madame G had told her. The Guardians in The Den liked their ladies willing, single, and forgettable. Undercover spies of Madame G's had studied the club and questioned the women who had been with the wolves. Each wolf did their own "thing" with the ladies. And the key to success was to wait for a night when there were three of them occupying a room in The Den.

It'd been quiet the last couple of weeks. Sigma worried their chance had passed and began brainstorming another route. Then tonight, two Guardians came in. A good sign, but it may not be enough to get the sample needed. Janice had gotten her sweet little ass over to the club as soon as the call came in from her contact.

There he was! A third Guardian known to frequent the same room as the other two, at the same time. Janice recognized him from the photos: tall, of course, with shoulder-length dark hair, a hawk-like nose and strong jawline. He was big, built like a weightlifter. Oh, she wanted to see what he had to offer. The other two Guardians were fine specimens: tall, powerfully built, and magazine cover gorgeous. This was her first foray into shifter sex and she couldn't think of any three better to kick it off with.

She stood up and straightened her skirt, which wasn't too loose and definitely not too tight. She wore subdued heels so she didn't scream desperate and a light teal bra underneath a see-through billowy shirt that overlapped her skirt to help camouflage the pockets sewn into the skirt and what she had in them.

Janice sauntered up to Mason, seeing the other two wolves had taken a young blonde thing back a few minutes ago. It would be perfect timing if Mason was joining in on the legendary shifter orgies in The Den.

"Hey," she purred, stirring her drink and taking a sip.

Mason turned, his dark eyes watching her mouth close on the straw before they burned a path down her body and back up to her face.

Her hair was not a natural red, but it looked natural the way she had it done. Blondes may get the first looks, but redheads intrigued men. She knew how to fix her hair and makeup so men would look at her and think sex, not hooker, which she most definitely was not. She was a sexual artist. She spent her life teaching female recruits how to be the same and showing the males what to watch for—and what to do when their prey took the bait.

"Hey, yourself," Mason drawled.

***

It worked! After a few minutes of chit chat, Mason led her to the back room in The Den where the other two wolves were already occupied with their play.

Mason grabbed her up in a hungry kiss. She could've told him that he didn't need to shield her from what they'd see when they entered the room. It only made her more excited.

She kissed him back and wrapped her legs around him when he grabbed her ass. He opened the door with his shoulder, carried her through and leaned her back against the door to shut it when they entered.

The club's music was slightly more muted in the room, and the only other sounds were flesh slapping flesh, a woman moaning, and male grunts. Janice was immediately wet.

Holding her against the door, the shifter called Mason moved one hand around to thumb her sex. She moved against it, breaking contact with his mouth only to breathe, "Take me, please."

Feeling how ready she already was (easy to do since she didn't wear underwear), he grabbed her ass again and carried her over to a chair next to the door.

Mason set on the edge of the chair while kneeling down, leaned her back, and moved her knees up and out to the side. Her chest heaving, she watched him, waiting. He dipped his head down and tongued her. Janice sighed and leaned all the way back to enjoy the ride. He held her knees while he expertly licked and suckled at her. It took sixty seconds for her first orgasm hit fast and hard.

Then he reared up, flipped open his fly with one hand while ripping a condom pack open with his teeth. He was still rolling the condom on when he entered and started thrusting. Janice was getting into the rhythm when he withdrew and went back down on her. He continued that pattern of licking, then thrusting, for three more orgasms when he finally slammed inside her and groaned.

Janice didn't want the pleasure to end, but she was ready to get on with her mission. When he pulled out to deal with the condom, she put on her most sultry look, and moved forward running her hands down him, grabbing his hands to help pull her forward. She used that distraction to take care of the condom herself. He watched her through half-lidded eyes as she palmed his balls with one hand while rolling it off the rest of the way.

She stood, keeping eye contact, and walked to the sink to throw it. Right before she reached the wastebasket, she used the pocket-picking skills Sigma recruits taught her to switch his used condom out with the empty, unused one stashed in her skirt pocket.

Then she turned, and leaned against the sink, biting her lip. The other two wolves, one as blond as the other was exotically dark, had finished with the first girl and escorted her out. Mason watched her, waiting to see if she was willing to satisfy them. She was. Her mission wasn't done yet, after all. Mason was just for fun, a way in to reach her target.

Janice left Mason to choose another participant and sauntered over to the others. The dark-haired one, the one with eyes that gleamed like liquid mercury, dropped into his chair and slid forward, his member jutting up. He grabbed a condom out of the jumbo box on the end table and rolled it over himself. She licked her lips and dropped to her knees before him. The blond did the same behind her, running his hands down her backside as he leaned over her and grabbed a condom for himself.

She gripped the large man's thigh as she wrapped her hand around the base of his shaft and slowly, sensually licked the tip while seductively catching his gaze. She temporarily lost her nerve. Except for the need to release driving him, his eyes were empty, void. No desire, no passion, definitely not tenderness. He didn't see her. She was just a mouth. Even the vamps she kept satisfied and the recruits she seduced on a regular basis made her feel like more than a toy to be used and discarded. But at the training facility she had a certain level of power over them, she was either their food source and they had to earn the right to feed off her by pleasuring her, or she was their instructor, one they must heed and obey.

Fortunately, the one from behind ran his hand through her slickness and she rocked into him, letting the sensations take over, as she took the male in front of her deeper into her mouth. He was so big, his width making it difficult to fit much. She used her hand as much as she could to bring him release. It was imperative she please this one, her mission hinged on it.

She moaned as she was eased into from behind, his size as impressive as Mason's. All the rumors she'd heard about shifters, especially the Guardians, were true. Once he settled fully into her wet channel, he committed to a steady driving rhythm which she matched with her mouth and hands on the other male.

She allowed the pleasure sweep through her and do what she did best. She gave all she had to the dark-haired male who let his eyes fall shut and dropped his head back as he rocked his hips under her. She used the force of the thrusts from behind to power her rhythm. As her center tightened, the pleasure growing, she worked his length fiercely.

She felt the blond male pick up his pace, his grunts coming faster, his pounding harder. Her orgasm built until she couldn't hold it back, afraid they'd quit, thinking she was done before she could secure the seed she needed. She cried out, the sound's vibrations running down the length of the male in her mouth, sending him over the edge, hot ejaculate filling the condom in her mouth. The male pumping behind her came as well, leaning over her back, breathing heavy.

When he pulled out from behind, that was her cue. Using the same provocative look that worked with Mason, she rolled the condom off him and stood up. She deliberately avoided the other male as he was cleaning up himself and followed the same plan as before with disposal. Except, this time she switched out the used condom from Mason to throw away and carefully pocketed the used condom from the male she gave a blow job to. It was his seed, "product" Sigma called it, that was critical to the mission.

The network knew the wolves that used The Den were very particular about their bodily fluids. They used protection religiously, always provided it, and burned it when the night was over. It didn't used to be that way. Human STDs crossing to paras weren't a concern, and neither were unplanned pregnancies. It was urban myth in the para world that any conception could occur outside mated couples in both the vampire and shifter world, but everyone heard stories. Whether it was true or not, no one knew. Tales of experiments by Sigma and Madame G capturing shifters and what she did to them kept the species guarding their genetics religiously.

Once he heard the slight weight of the condom hit the trash, the stunning blond with the movie star looks came up behind her, rubbing his hands up and down her arms.

"Come on, sweet thing. Let's go find your friends," he murmured softly.

She looked up at him in the mirror, ready to rely on her flirtatious skills, and paused. He may be the charmer, the one picking the girls so the dark, brooding one wouldn't terrify them with his coldness, but there was nothing but script in his face: no feeling, no emotion, little caring. Everything this male said, every move he made with any of these women, including her, was scripted. He didn't see them, she doubted he even knew their names. Hell, she didn't know theirs, either.

Janice leaned back against the sink—her legs felt like jelly—and saw Mason working on another girl, a brunette this time. A loud one. The scents of arousal, sex, and need hung in the air like a haze, her clit started to throb again. Her goal was complete; shifter seed in her pocket. Once this mission was done, there was no coming back here for her.

She looked up through her eyelashes and met the male's navy blue eyes in the mirror. "I don't have any friends here, but I do have more time."

Chapter Nine

Their first official date, he picked her up on time. The doorbell rang and when she opened the door, she melted at the appraising look he gave her. His hot gaze swept over her all the way down to her gladiator sandals, where it burned even hotter as he slowly followed her body back up her capris and empire-waist blouse to her face. His diamond eyes glittered, nearly glowing.

It took her longer to make it past his lips, enjoying his reaction to her. She always wore sensible clothes, nothing ostentatious, flashy, or trashy. But he made her feel like he'd never seen anything sexier than department store apparel. As she captured her own surreptitious perusal of him, she was surprised he wasn't wearing all black. Before, he came off as the ultimate bad boy. But dressed in blue jeans and a heather gray button-down with his standard motorcycle boots, he was an attainable bad boy—the kind a girl thought she could change.

Nerves threatened to overtake her stomach again. They'd been plaguing her all day. Where would he take her? How awkward would it be? Would they even go out or barely make it past her door like last time? At least tonight, it wouldn't look like the local biker gang was trolling bank tellers for dates. Tonight, with him standing on her doorstep, ringing her doorbell, she accepted they could be a believable couple.

That was until she followed him out to her driveway.

"What. Is. That?" she asked

"My bike."

"When you said dress casual, I didn't think you meant 'wear all leather so you don't end up as roadkill.'"

He reached for her hand, wrapping it in his, leading her to his large steel monstrosity.

"I even got a helmet for you," he said, as if that were the perfect balm for her frazzled nerves.

"And the rest of my body?" She dubiously eyed the intimidating piece of machinery. She should've known his mode of transportation was on wheels of death.

He chuckled. "Trust me, Tinkerbell. Once you relax enough to enjoy the ride, you'll wonder why you don't ride every day. Nothing else makes you feel as alive and free."

He hadn't called her Tinkerbell since *that* night. The term of endearment warmed her, calming the storm in her belly that threatened to send her back into her house, dead-bolting the door.

Jace leaned down close and said, "But until you relax, feel free to hold onto me as tightly as you'd like." He winked at her. Winked! Did he not think

she had serious hang-ups about going anywhere
with him on that thing at any speed?

He pulled out a shiny red helmet and helped her
put it on. "We'll stay in town and get some dinner,
then drive down by the river. We'll stay off the
highways. Promise."

Cassie reluctantly climbed on the back.
"Where's your helmet?" she grumbled. He climbed
on in front of her, his broad shoulders blocking her
view. Unable to resist, she leaned into him, his scent
and heat comforting.

"We heal fast. Unless I lose my head, or my
heart, I'll be okay."

"*Hello?* Those injuries have been known to
happen with motorcycle accidents."

He reached back to grab her arms, wrapping
them around his middle. "Injuries, yes. We'll heal,
unless they're gone entirely. Now hang on." With
that, he fired up the engine and they were off.

The first several minutes were terrifying, but as
she moved with the turns, felt his enjoyment being
"alive and free", and relaxed into him, she realized
he had been right. When he pulled up to the cottage
café, she was almost disappointed they'd arrived
already. She missed her arms wrapped around him,
hands gripping his hard abs.

They chatted casually all through dinner. He
talked fondly about his family, pangs of loss and
regret were evident, but it was clear he had come to
terms with the situation and respected his mom and

sister's wishes. He asked about her and she tiptoed around her upbringing.

"Basically, I had an idyllic life up until I was ten. Then my mom passed away from cancer, my dad went crazy with grief and quit taking his meds, so the state took me away and locked him up. Thus, the fostered daughter of a schizophrenic dad went into the mental health profession," she said plainly, hoping he'd leave it at that.

He gave her a considering look, "What do you do, exactly?"

She couldn't help but give him a grateful look for asking about work rather than her father. She loved her dad. He was doing better and they'd repaired their relationship, but her past was hard to talk about. It made her wonder what if he relapsed again, could she lose him again? "I work with clinic patients, not inpatients. Adults, no kids, and I focus more on mental disorders, mainly arising from childhood trauma. The majority of my patients are transitioning from inpatient stays to learning to function in real world settings."

"It must be very rewarding work."

Cassie shrugged and replied, "It's interesting." She took a sip of her water. "So what do you do besides bartend and ride a motorcycle?"

"I go to school."

Cassie raised her eyebrows and quickly tried to cover her shock. She didn't want him to think she thought he was an ambitionless ex-con with no future plans in life. She totally didn't... really.

"What are you going to school for?"

"Business, an MBA." He looked away a bit sheepishly. "I worked on my bachelor's in prison. Nothing else to do with all that time."

Fearing her eyebrows would never come down, her hot bartender had rendered her speechless. He was embarrassed to have to bring up his prison stint even though he'd worked on self-improvement. He could have been in-your-face smug knowing she, someone who studied people for a living, assumed he barely passed high school.

"So what did you study?" She wanted to learn more about the real him and not the Jace he presented to the world.

"Business and accounting. Figured it could take me anywhere. But I came back here," he spread his hands wide and leaned back into his chair, "found Christian and got a job doing his books during the day, stocking and tending bar at night."

"Found Christian? Did you know him from before?"

Jace shook his head. "No, just had heard of him. He's become a pack leader for the area. For those of us who are essentially packless."

"And that means?"

"Wolves have packs. If you leave one, you can be accepted into another one and abide by their rules and regulations. If you're estranged, then you lack the resources our kind sometimes needs— protection, new identities, hiding in plain sight.

"Christian was an alpha, left his pack for his wife, Mabel, and moved here. He's been able to reinvent himself consistently over the years. He seems to attract rogue alphas with no home, puts them to work, takes care of any problems, and we stay content to have a place to set down and live a little. He's become pack leader for the West Creek area."

"You're an alpha?" She was not surprised in the least.

"Yeah, I would've been." He said no more, not wanting to delve into that part of his past again. He finished up his drink and stood, offering her his hand. "Ready for a scenic ride?"

She grinned, begrudgingly, and accepted his hand, standing.

The ride was beautiful, the evening air crisp and refreshing. The hum of the bike lulled her, her earlier fear of riding gone. He took them down a side road through the trees paralleling the river, but true to his word, turned around to head back into town when the road's speed limits increased. She sat behind him, helmet firmly in place, and sank into his back, enjoying the view and the feel of him.

***

Jace pulled off the road into a riverfront park before they got back to town. Large, shading cottonwoods dotted the shore, monuments detailing the area's history were adjacent to the walking path, interspersed with benches to sit and enjoy the peace of the great outdoors.

Cassie took Jace's hand while climbing off and held onto it while he led her toward one of the benches.

"This place is almost always empty toward evening. I thought we could hang for a bit before I took you back." Jace hoped she didn't mind.

Cassie closed her eyes briefly to breathe in the fresh river air. "It's lovely. Do you come here often?"

"When I'm studying and the bar is too loud to concentrate." Jace picked a bench facing the river so they could watch the early season boaters go by. He sat with his arm across the back of the bench behind her, hoping she'd snuggle in next to him. And she did. With his heightened senses, he didn't have to lean down to inhale her scent. The subtle floral and vanilla aroma worked its way through his body, easing his worry about her still possible rejection of him. At the same time, it brought the memories of the stronger version of those scents in her office and what he'd done with her the one and only time he'd ever been to her office.

He tried to redirect his thoughts before his raging erection captured her attention, potentially ruining their compatible evening. He made it through the long ride, when her arms were wrapped around him, her delightful breasts pressed against his back, where they brought to mind the details of their size and shape. He remembered the rosy tips perfectly, and how they peaked when his mouth got so close—*Fuck!* Need to make more conversation.

"You look great." He hoped the desire clouding his gruff voice wasn't obvious.

"Thanks. You too, as always."

"You've been checking me out?" he teased.

Cassie chuckled. "Maybe a little." She reached up and feathered her fingers over his scalp. "Do you have to shave your head every day?"

Jace stilled. Cassie snatched her hand back, sensing the sudden tension.

"I'm sorry," she said, quickly.

"No, it's just—I didn't want…" He drifted off, gathering his thoughts. "I intend to tell you everything eventually. I do. I just didn't want the low points in my life to cloud our getting to know each other, like they did at first."

Cassie nodded, her dark eyes were filled with concern and a little dread, so he figured he'd just get on with it before her imagination, combined with what she already knew and had witnessed, got the best of her.

"One of the convicts in prison, one of Madame G's fucked up experiments, knew what I was. He was relentless, fuck. Just fucking messing with me those first couple years—stealing my belongings, throwing my food tray across the room, whatever would make my life hell. They called him Argen, you know, a play off of argentum, the Latin word for silver."

"Why silver?"

"His teeth were capped with silver. He even had his nails embedded with silver. The old legends had that part right about werewolves: silver's deadly to shifters. One morning in the showers, his gang got to me. Held me down while he shaved me with a silver razor."

"So your hair won't grow back, just being cut by silver?" Cassie asked incredulously.

Jace nodded.

"And the scars on your shoulder? Argen?"

Jace nodded. "Wounds made from silver will scar. If we can treat the silver poisoning with salt, usually saline, everything else should heal completely."

"And then what?" Cassie prompted.

"And then I planned. I wasn't going to spend my years behind bars fighting Argen. Commander Fitzsimmons' contact found me. Argen was getting careless and we took him down before he revealed our secrets to the humans we lived among. I was pretty much left alone after that." Jace waited while Cassie thought over his revelation.

"So if you heal completely otherwise, then how do shifters have tattoos? Like yours covering your scars."

Jace let out a laugh, stunned at her line of conversation. She was either accepting their world, or avoiding it. "A special blend of ink with both silver dust and saline. I got mine as soon as I got out."

He watched her, snuggled into him, hoping she wouldn't do the ol' yawn-I'm-tired-let's-call-it-a-night. Her contemplative expression gazing out at the river told him she had more questions, but was unsure of whether to ask him. He didn't know whether to encourage her or dread another question.

"What's your power?" she finally asked.

The girl kept going left when he expected her to go right.

"My power?" He knew exactly what she meant, he just wanted to know what she knew.

"Well, at the risk of a HIPAA violation, I can't tell you how I heard many shifters have a special talent that goes beyond even a sixth sense."

Ah, Bennett told her. So she knew about their extra abilities, just not his, nor how he'd used it in the past. That could wait until she trusted him completely.

"I can persuade people to do what I want them to."

"That's handy."

"Sometimes. If they're really against what I'm asking, then it's difficult, sometimes impossible. The length of the effect is variable, depending on how strong someone's mind is." Cassie gazed across the river again. He could read her easier now, and if she wasn't looking at him, then she was processing something that made her uncomfortable. "And no, I have never, and will never, use it on you."

Finally, she looked up and met his eyes again with a shy smile. "What do you use it for?"

"You mean other than booking an appointment with a hot doctor?" Jace watched the slight blush stain her cheeks as she recalled their "appointment", loving that she was not unaffected when reminded how explosive they were together. "Usually to prevent trouble, their purpose being to keep our species safe. I used it in prison to get the other inmates and guards to leave me alone. It worked really well after Argen was gone. Now, I mostly use it to talk people out of stupid fights at the bar."

Cassie settled in a little closer. He wrapped his arm around her a little tighter, trailing his fingers up and down her skin, content to hold her. Mostly. He wanted to do more with her, so much more, but now wasn't the time. She needed to get to know him, feel comfortable with him, learn to trust her instincts that told her they belonged together.

"Do you change often?" she asked a bit hesitantly.

"Every chance I get. Running through the woods is a great stress reliever and after so many years of being restricted, I crave the openness and the freedom. Saves on a gym membership," he joked. She had only witnessed the violent part of their shifter nature. He wanted her to understand they were as much a part of nature as they were the human world.

"I get it. I'm a runner, too, but I stick to asphalt paths. Too many strange, naked men running through the woods," she teased.

Jace laughed, enjoying their interplay. "You don't hear that part of the story in Little Red Riding Hood, where she sees the Big Bad Wolf's bare ass cuz his clothes are in a pile in the woods."

Cassie giggled and stood up, grabbing his hand and pulling him with her. "Come on. It's getting late. Let's go ride back to town and have some dessert."

Chapter Ten

They wandered up to Cassie's door, holding hands, fingers entwined. Cassie didn't want the night to end; she enjoyed dating Jace. He was warm, funny, intelligent, and gorgeous—gawd, he was hot.

When they reached their door, he turned to her and cupped her face. "This is where I kiss you goodnight," he murmured.

Giddy with anticipation, wishing he'd ask to bypass the dating deal and carry her into her bedroom where they could remain all night, she tilted her chin up to him as he leaned in.

He tasted divine. Still sweet from their shared dessert, fresh from their ride home, this one kiss made her feel more alive than zipping through the city streets on his steel monster.

She heard a subtle popping noise and Jace grunted. His perplexed brow creased and he slumped against her, sinking to his knees.

A small dart stuck out of his shoulder. Cassie struggled to keep him from face-planting on her concrete steps. "Jace, what is that? What's happening?"

Jace had his phone out, hitting a speed dial number before it clattered to the ground. "Get the Guardians," was all he mumbled before he lost consciousness.

She squatted next to Jace, her vision blurred and her thigh throbbed. A dart similar to Jace's was lodged into her muscle. Someone called out for Jace on the other end of his phone.

Cassie dropped back on her butt, sagging against Jace's still form. "We need help." She prayed the man on the phone heard and could help them.

A dark shadow fell across Cassie, the familiar form highlighted by the light above her door. Cassie's fuzzy mind registered a sort of déjà vu where she'd been on the ground, looking up at a powerful figure before her. *Alex?*

"Sorry, Runner Girl. Boss said it was time to take you in. She's got plans for you and your boo, there." It was the last thing she heard before she joined Jace in oblivion.

***

Jace's head fucking pounded. His mind tried to process why. Sensing Cassie nearby, he wondered if they crashed his bike. No, he remembered dropping her off. Did he have the strength to leave her place with nothing but a goodnight kiss? Wait, they were kissing, and then trepidation replaced confusion. He kept his eyes closed, listening to his surroundings.

Clean air carried on a light breeze that can only be found far away from the city surrounded him. The tangy scent of bark and budding trees meant they were in a wooded area.

Did his call to Christian go through? Fucking Sigma bastards. He knew they were in the area, a few recent cases of shifters suddenly going off the grid had the Guardians concerned Sigma's tendrils had sunk into West Creek. They would be the perfect group for Sigma to harvest from – they laid low, often with little family, even fewer friends. No one to miss them if they happened to disappear one day.

Why they targeted Jace and Cassie, he could only guess, and none of it good. They didn't throw surprise mating showers for lucky couples about to tie their lives together.

He opened his senses to listen for Cassie's breathing. Slow and steady suggesting she was still out cold. They must've hit her with a tranq, too. *Bastards!* His rage rose and he forced his breathing to remain even. His arms were tied in front of him, his legs bound at the ankles; hers must be, too.

"The male's aware," he heard a deep human voice say.

"Why don't you open those stunning eyes of yours and join us?" said a female shifter. Her tone was airy, like this was quite the rave he was missing out on. "Your honey's not up yet and we can't get started without her. And by the way, don't try the freaky eye thing on us. You can't capture more than one of us in your radar and we're not taking the bait."

He slowly opened his eyes, very little moonlight filtered through the newly-budding trees, it was well after sunset. He had no idea how long they'd been passed out, but from overhearing the Guardians talk training and weapons, he thought they said the tranqs could last a couple of hours. That was for a grown shifter male, what would they do to Cassie?

As if sensing his line of thought, the female continued, "Runner Girl should be coming around soon, we tapered her dose—weak human, and all."

"Fuck you, X," the male human swore.

"Please, Double D, don't be so sensitive," she replied. "I know it's not your fault you're human."

The male continued cursing under his breath.

The use of letters as names told him a lot, along with their knowledge of what he could do. A sick feeling sunk into the pit of his belly. That sadistic bitch, Madame G, liked to keep her Agents' names shortened to a letter. She took recruits, or anyone she took a fancy to, snatched them up and broke them down, rebuilding them to her liking through pain and terror, and whatever sadistic act she happened to think would "develop character." Then she named them with a letter in case it wasn't already obvious she owned them.

He assessed the area, only his eyes moved. They were deep in the woods, probably on the east side of the river, since he didn't recognize the general scent of the land. He'd run in the woods surrounding West Creek, but rarely crossed over to Freemont. The larger city made it harder to get lost in nature. More people were building out of town and it took longer to get lost in the wilderness on all fours. He could head out for a run from his apartment above Pale Moonlight, strip down at the edge of town, and shift to finish his run in the woods. It was commonplace for Christian's pack to run. No humans thought much beyond the initial thrill when they saw a lone wolf in the trees, if they ever saw them. Great care was taken by them all to remain undetected. It was better that way.

Cassie had begun to squirm and groan, stiff from being bound, her head pounding.

"Hey, look who's joining us!" X said brightly. Her tone dropped to a grave timber. "Call Madame G. It's time," she ordered Agent D.

"Alex? Jace?" Cassie groggily inquired. Alex? Did she know this Sigma drone?

"Boo-bear is next to you, awaiting the special ceremony we have in store. Oh, and call me X. I use Alex when I'm trying to blend. It was great running with you Cass-bass. You gotta great set of legs, for a human."

Cassie's look of betrayal toward the female made the animal inside Jace howl. She met Jace's gaze, fear quickly replacing betrayal, he could feel his wolf pacing, growing increasingly agitated, but a shift now wouldn't help either of them. The reality of the situation was sinking into both of them. X had been watching them, studying her, even made contact and chatted her up to screen for information.

Cassie took a deep breath and gathered her wits, making Jace proud. His mate had been drugged, woke up bound in the woods, in the middle of the night, and hadn't crumbled yet.

"I'm at a disadvantage, obviously," Cassie said evenly, meeting X's bright green eyes. "I'm human, and you are?"

"Like your boyfriend," she replied simply. "But worry not, Little Boo, you're not alone. Double D, here, is human, too. Just a bit more enhanced."

Cassie and Jace both searched for "Double D." He had dark hair, dark eyes, and dark stubble covered a face that had anger clouding it. Jace didn't know why X taunted her partner, but it was obvious he didn't like it and he didn't like her. Jace inhaled deep, scenting two more human males in the surrounding woods. Their scents were more subtle than Double D's, but more "enhanced" than your run-of-the-mill *Homo sapiens*.

"So you're a shifter and you hunt your own kind?" Cassie asked innocuously.

Jace monitored X's face carefully. No emotions flickered across, her expression carefully impassive. "Madame G can be very persuasive," she said flatly. "Much like your boyfriend can be, you should ask your ex. Grant, right? Sudden lack of interest in sex before marriage? Hmmm… suddenly dumped? Hmmm…"

Jace ground his jaw and met Cassie's wide-eyed accusatory stare. "I would never use my gift on you, but I will use it *for* you."

She continued to hold her stare, but gave her head a shake of incredulous incomprehension.

X laughed caustically. "Boo, I'll give it to you. That's some manipulative shit. Seriously, though, it's nice to see there's a shifter around here that has a handle on his mojo. The Guardians of the W. C.? I tell ya. It shouldn't have been so easy to settle in the area, but with them and their fucked up powers dealing with all the pack rejects that gravitate here and can't live under the radar? Easy peasy lemon squeasy."

Jace mentally filed away everything X was saying. If—when—they got out of here alive, he'd bring it all in to Commander Fitzsimmons. Rumors abounded of Sigma activity increasing in the area, but did the Guardians know they were digging in their tentacles deep? He knew they were busy with the drama kicked up by the shifters in the area, but Jace had also heard whispers that their heavy-handed techniques were compensating for discrepant powers, ones they couldn't control or just plain didn't work.

A tall Asian beauty appeared out of thin air, covered neck to toe in a black kimono with blood-red serpent designs flowing over the material, her features marred with cruelty and amusement. She greedily looked over Cassie and Jace, like they were the new Keurig coffee maker with eighty different flavors she couldn't wait to test.

"Get them to the altar. Let's begin."

Jace prepped to turn, his wolf wanting to take out this woman whom he only sensed malignant evil from, when X stopped him. "I wouldn't, Boo. There's one sniper trained on you and one on Runner Girl. We'd only wound her for now, unless you two prove not worth the effort. Either way, if you or she fights back, it'll get ugly. Now get up, both of you."

Jace blew out the breath he didn't know he was holding, the fight leaving him... temporarily. Cassie was in this because of him, he would only ensure her safety from now on. She was all that was important.

She looked at him with fear in her eyes as she struggled to her knees, bits of grass and leaves stuck to her clothes and hair. Her pixie-cut, decorated with small twigs and bits of leaves, made her look like a wee woodland fairy. Rising ungracefully to his feet, the task more arduous since his bound hands were connected by a short chain to his bound ankles, he wished fervently that Cassie could fly, while he shifted and took on the wolf bitch, and her human minions. And Madame G, whatever the fuck she was. Vampire, but something else. Something dark that he didn't recognize. Whiffs coming off her were familiar to him. Like the rare, truly evil prisoners he came across doing time. Like Argen— the ones that could never be rehabilitated because if there was such a thing as a black soul, they had it. They were completely devoid of humanity, viewing those around them as pawns for their own malicious use.

They hobbled over to the pile of stones that signified the "altar." An altar for what, Jace dreaded finding out. Madame G stood tall and regal atop the loosely stacked stones. Behind her, a short distance away, Jace's enhanced night vision could barely make out a small shack sitting among the trees. He wondered what Cassie could make out with her rudimentary human vision. Grays and blacks? Shadowy figures moving around her? She had to be absolutely fucking terrified.

A breeze rustled through the branches, making it difficult for Jace to determine where the snipers were, or separate their scents and figure just how many were out there in addition to the twisted woman on the rocks and the traitor wolf, X, with pissed off Agent D behind them. The need to keep Cassie safe, both drove the wolf wild and crazy, wanting to kill everyone around him to save her, but calming it down knowing any hint of him shifting would cause her harm.

Once they were a few feet in front of the altar, Agent D ordered them to stop and kneel. Cassie hesitated slightly and Agent D shoved behind her knees causing her to drop with a cry.

Jace growled, turning to lunge at the bastard when X fired a shot into the ground in front of Cassie.

"Jace!" Cassie's eyes were wide, fear running rampant through her.

"Kneel, Jace," X commanded calmly, moonlight reflecting off the gunmetal pointed at Cassie. "Remember my advice? That was your only warning shot. Next time, it's in her leg."

Cassie trembled, breathing shallowly as he kneeled down next to her.

"Don't touch her again, Double D, or I will take you down," Jace threatened.

Agent D rammed the butt of his revolver into the back of Jace's head making him grunt in pain. He leaned down close to Jace's ear, "It's Agent D, and I'd like to see you try, wolf. I'd skin you alive in front of your pretty little lady and wear your fur like a mantle."

Jace sought out Cassie's terrified, watery gaze to help calm her. He nodded slightly to reassure her he was okay since he couldn't reach out to comfort her, hoping they were close enough that she would catch the movement. She swallowed hard and gave a small nod back.

"Mmmm, you'd better watch it. Double D doesn't like his name being fucked up," X taunted wryly, giving Jace a wink since her back was to Madame G. Apparently, there was no love lost between Agent X and Agent D.

"Enough." Madame G daintily stepped down from her stone perch, the long kimono barely shifting as it moved over the rocks, holding an intricate blade in her pale, finely-boned hand. The hilt was decorated with an obscene amount of jewels that valued enough to buy the club. Hell, buy the whole block. She was running her red claw-tipped fingers lovingly up and down the blade. Jace longed to snap each delicate finger and thrill in the agony that would replace the cold delight in her expression.

The wind flowed around Madame G when she covered the short distance between them. The long ponytail atop her head swayed gently with her movements but no wind touched her; her footsteps made no sound—no crunching of dry leaves, no snapping of old twigs, nothing. She stopped, looming tall and dark over them, the moonlight streaming down behind her but illuminating nothing around her.

"You two are at a very special place in your relationship. You will share it with me." She nodded to Agent D. "Their hands."

X stood with a revolver in each hand, one trained on Jace and one on Cassie, while Agent D released one of each of their hands, the ones closest to each other, from the bindings in front of them. Jace's feeling of dread, which was bad before, multiplied. Times one hundred.

"Now hold hands," Madame G commanded.

Needing no more encouragement, Cassie desperately grabbed onto Jace's hand, twining her fingers tightly through his. He let her cool fingers snake through his before clasping onto her just as tightly. She had no idea what was going to happen next, but Jace now knew exactly what Madame was going to do. The most sacred act that could take place between two shifters would be forcibly performed on them. It would be twisted and studied for Madame G's benefit. It made sense now, why the evil creature herself, the one he'd begun to think of as an urban legend, a nighttime story to scare the young into being good, came to their abduction, instead of letting her revered Agents carry it out.

"Very good," cooed Madame G, her dark eyes reflecting a fire that did not exist on this plane. She leaned forward, reaching one claw-tipped hand out to grip their hands and wedge her thumb between their palms. Cassie attempted to break free, Jace tried to let go of her hand but Madame G's freakishly strong hold kept them tightly together.

He was leaning his body away, frantically using the extra force to rip apart their hands when Madame G dropped the dagger in where her thumb was and twisted it back out, slicing both of their hands at once.

Cassie and Jace both hissed in pain, warm blood welled out from between their palms, but even without Madame G's vice grip, their hands wouldn't break apart.

Madame G began chanting, her words unintelligible, the wind ominously picked up, pushing through the trees, making them wheeze and rasp all around them. Her low timbre picked up volume; she flung her head back and held the bloodied blade up to the sky, her voice rising with the strength of the wind. Old leaves kicked up around them still on their knees, swirling high into the air, disappearing into darkness.

"What's happening?" Cassie cried to Jace, the wind tearing the words from her.

Jace couldn't answer her, didn't know how to tell her, what to tell her.

X's eyes never wavered, her guns still trained on each of them. Not that they had any power to move. Ever since Madame G touched their bare skin, it felt like they were cemented into place, every major muscle paralyzed. He couldn't shield Cassie from the torment of the wind and leaves, couldn't snatch the dagger from Madame G and plunge it into her black heart, couldn't rip Agent D apart for shoving Cassie, and couldn't take on X for tricking and betraying his mate. Jace always took care of his own, those most precious to him, even at great cost to himself. And now he made a solemn vow. *We will survive and I will dedicate my life to destroying Madame G and her Sigma network so they can never spread their terror and ruination over my species ever again.*

The vacuum of the mini-cyclone sucked the air from their vicinity making it difficult to breathe. Madame G's voice rose until she was nearly screaming at the sky. With one final shout, the wind died suddenly when Madame G brought the blade down to her lips. Her eyelids dropped closed when her pointed, strawberry tongue deftly licked both sides, her mouth curling up at the corners. Jace winced; Cassie gagged.

In the sudden silence that followed, Madame G said, "I pronounce you, husband and wife."

***

They could move now. Cassie clung to Jace's bloodied hand. What the fuck was this crazy lady talking about?

"D, bring my box," Madame G commanded.

Agent D appeared in front of them with an ornate, long box. Madame G laid the dagger down into it and shut the lid.

"Keep this with you and see them settled." Her vacuous, dark eyes stained Cassie's soul whenever they settled on her. Cassie watched in astonishment as Madame G disappeared into the wind right before her eyes.

"What happened?" she breathed to Jace.

Jace's face was grim, he gave her hand a squeeze, prepared to say something when X interrupted. "Congrats. You're mated! Sorry, I didn't bring any confetti and champagne, but don't worry. We have a nice room for you two lovebirds all set up so you can get some mating on." She winked again and spoke quietly into a radio.

"So you can rut like the dogs you are," sneered Agent D.

Jace tensed and loosened his fist, ready to spring at the Agent who clearly hated shifters and anyone associated with them. Cassie squeezed Jace's hand even harder, refusing to let him go, urging him not to react. Her heart raced faster than she thought possible. *Mated? This isn't right. It doesn't feel right.*

"Rise my little lovebirds," X delighted. "Boo, I'm sure you can make out the honeymoon suite up ahead. That is your new vacation destination for the next couple of days. All you two need to do is bask in the glow of new matehood and we'll provide the rest."

Now that Madame G was gone, her presence no longer leaching any light from her personal space, Cassie could make out people and shapes slightly better. The moon was still up, having lost much luster to the approaching dawn. Agent X still had her weapons trained on the kneeling pair, increasing Cassie's feeling of diffidence around these beings. Jace had heightened strength and power, but any hint that he was about to unleash his beast and Cassie would pay the price. Yet she couldn't defend herself against the female shifter, who not only had the advantage of being armed, but may be just as strong and capable as Jace when in wolf form. Then, there was the man X referred to in bra size, ratcheting his ire and hatred of all things lupine, who seemed to revel in their demise. And if X wasn't lying, there were more Agents in the surrounding woods to keep these tenebrous proceedings on track.

"Yo, Double D," X called, tucking one of her sidearms back into its holster. "Hold on tight to that box. We wouldn't want that thing to plunge into one their hearts. We can't have mating take backs."

"Fuck you, X," Agent D returned back to her. "Do your job and I'll do mine." Followed by a "four-legged bitch" under his breath.

"I heard you," X sang and burst out laughing, no doubt peaking Agent D's anger with her.

Great, getting kidnapped by two letters that hated each other. No wonder they were on the opposite ends of the alphabet.

Cassie looked around her, probing the darkness for the honeymoon suite. Jace adroitly rose to his feet, anger and unease emanating from him as he bent to help Cassie to hers. She struggled to her feet with the assistance of her mate, clinging to him for any small measure of comfort. They each only had one hand free, the rest of their limbs shackled together, but Jace wrapped that arm protectively around her waiting for instruction.

"Move." Agent D shoved Jace's shoulder with enough force that Cassie would have been sprawled on her face. Jace barely budged, a low growl rumbling through his chest.

Agent D was about to snarl again, looking for another reason to hit either of them, but X cut him off. "Double D," X chided, "it's not very amorous for the happy couple to get accosted before their consummation."

Like she and Jace could get lost in a lover's embrace after that foul ceremony? What was X thinking? Cassie stepped forward, forgetting her connected ankles, suddenly afraid she'd break her free wrist when she hit the ground.

Jace snatched her up before she made contact and swung her up to cradle her, tolerably able to use his bound arm to hold her, but it didn't seem to impede his ability. She clung to him as much as she was able, while he lurched forward in his slow stuttering step toward the small building she could now make out in the early dawn glow.

"It'll be all right, Cassie," Jace quietly reassured her. "I'll take care of you until we get out of here."

X let out a sharp bark of laughter. "You bet you'll take care of her. We gave her a little candy while she was out. It should be hitting soon. Then she'll need to be taken care of good and hard."

Jace's growl rumbled into her body. "What does that mean?" Cassie whispered.

"It means," X replied, as Cassie's whisper was more than enough for the woman's keen hearing, "that Madame G had us roofie you. It's her own special concoction she uses when she feels one of the intimate parties may not be as participatory as she'd like. She wants what she wants when she wants it, and she wants a mated couple fucking like rabbits 'til they produce young."

Cassie's insides ran cold. There was so much about what X said that disturbed her. First, she was drugged on top of being drugged. Next, she was being locked up with her date and expected to perform. And how would they know? Take their word for it? *Yep, we went at it like teenagers on prom night when their parents are out of town.* Nope. These people would watch. It was disturbing, but not as disturbing as what that evil mistress would want with a baby.

Jace reached the small wooden shack. It wasn't as rundown as Cassie originally imagined. Did they build it so far out here where they could escape, but get nowhere fast? Where no one could bear witness to the maniacal ceremony that had just been performed? X opened the door and stood back waiting for Jace to carry her over the threshold. This was so not what she expected for her wedding night. Jace was so *who* she did not expect for her wedding night. But as he carried her into the shack, his strong arms holding her tightly to him, giving her a modicum of security, he felt more right than Grant ever did. *He* felt more right, but not the sick, oily feeling that settled in her chest when they were mated.

Jace remained silent as he slid her down his body, ensuring she could stand without tipping over but not letting her go. X said an unknown word that sounded like a command and their bindings dropped to the ground then slid back toward the doorway to X's booted feet. Suddenly free, Cassie tensed, wondering if Jace would choose now to act. X must've been waiting for that, too. She remained still, an eyebrow raised in question toward him while he gave her a contemptuous stare-down in return. Agent D remained behind X, leering in on them, reminding Cassie what they were expected to do.

When it was clear that Jace would not be causing immediate trouble, X looked down to Cassie, her tone serious. "The candy we gave you has a bit of a delay, then you'll start getting really uncomfortable. You'll feel like you need to get off like you need to breathe."

Cassie gave X an impertinent look. So she would die of embarrassment and humiliation throwing herself at Jace while these monsters monitored the situation and ate popcorn. All she needed to do was trust Jace with the sanctity of her body, which she'd done several times since the night he brought her home. She wasn't worried about getting pregnant. Had Madame G never heard of the Depo shot? It would be months before she was fertile. She just needed to worry about how she and Jace would get out alive before Sigma realized producing a child wasn't happening this weekend, and either keep them longer or dispose of them.

Reading the lack of concern on Cassie's face, X continued. "The hormonal stimulant Madame G included will spur ovulation and augment your mating pheromones. Your scent will drive Boo out of his mind."

Blood drained out of Cassie's face and she felt light-headed. Jace swore under his breath. Agent D continued to leer at them, while Cassie interpreted sympathy in X's somber expression. As serious as she had been while relaying the devastating information, there was a hint, just a hint that only another female would pick up on, of compassion—a kindred spirit. Like X knew exactly what Cassie would go through; how her body would turn traitorous; how she would be at the mercy of the nearest male; and how the humiliation would settle in as unknown spectators would bear witness to it all. X said Madame G could be very persuasive and Cassie had only seen a dusting of her depravity in the last couple of hours. How long had X been under her supremacy?

"Just remember, Boo," X looked back up to Jace to deliver another warning, "even if you do manage to resist your urges and keep Cassie from jumping on your dick, she's still a shifter's mate. Madame G might just see if she will produce young for other shifters. It's been rumored to happen. She'll keep you to study and keep Cassie for blood feeding."

"That bitch can fucking try," Jace growled emphatically. "I will kill anyone who touches Cassie."

"You'd be… busy. We have a couple of female vamps, and they do love a good shifter meal. You know what their bite is like, right? Instant Viagra. The ol' fuck-and-suck and then they'd kill you. What is it with vampires versus werewolves, anyway? Any-hoodles, I'll tell the men outside to give y'all a little privacy and not watch too much. Only go in orifices, not out any; the doors and windows have sensors that'll alert the snipers."

As X turned to leave, she glanced at Cassie, regret flickered across her face so quickly Cassie could've sworn it was an illusion, then back to Jace. She spoke so quietly, Cassie almost didn't catch it. "Take care of her, Jace."

The use of Jace's actual name by X, sent a cold shiver of fear through Cassie. The use of nicknames gave X an aura of being aloof, maybe a little mischievous, causing people to underestimate her and let their feelings about what she called them influence their perception of the Agent. She might look like a rocker girl with her crazy black hair done up today in a messy faux hawk, but she worked for Madame G. And if Cassie wasn't mistaken, she was a high-ranking Agent, the leader of tonight's operation. X stalked Cassie, engaged her in friendly conversation, knew her routines and when she was out with Jace, and carried out the drugging and kidnapping of two full-sized adults in the middle of West Creek. Not to mention, the formidable female looked like she was built for strength and power. X was not to be underestimated.

The door closed and deadbolts *thunked* into place.

"Was she telling the truth? Was that mating?" Cassie hissed quietly.

"That wasn't mating," Jace said with derision. "That was an abomination of our ceremony." Then his voice softened, "But yes, we are mated. Can't you feel it?" He looked searchingly at her, waiting for her reaction.

"It doesn't feel right."

Jace looked away. She didn't mean to hurt him, but couldn't he feel the wrongness of it all?

She took advantage of the free use of her limbs and wandered around the small shack. It was a small, square room with one window that had bars. The walls were bare and there was no furniture aside from a mattress with a ratty gray blanket and bucket meant to be used as a chamber pot. They were supposed to have sex in this stark, stale room... on a doleful strip of cotton that probably saw plenty bodily fluids in its day with Sigma. This could be the Four Seasons, it wasn't happening.

Warmth flooded Cassie's groin, flashing quickly up her body, until her face was flushed crimson and breathing quickened to panting.

She gasped, "Oh, shit!"

Chapter Eleven

J ace felt the heat radiating from Cassie as she
paced frantically, hitting each wall, doing an
about face, and aiming for another wall, like a
caged… wolf.

"What are we going to do?" Cassie said, for
what must have been the fiftieth time. He'd tried
soothing her, but any movement toward her sent her
careening to another wall like a pinball. Anything
he said up to that point hadn't gotten through to her.
Her emotions were running too high, her hormones
in flux, and the information bombs X dropped on
them before she left pegged Cassie's calm meter.

Hands held up at his sides to show he didn't
intend to make any physical contact, he said,
"Cassie you need to stop and listen to me." She
needed to hear how he wouldn't take advantage of
her, that they could wait it out until there was a
moment to act, to get free. But the men outside, no
doubt listening, probably live-streaming them,
didn't need to hear that.

"What would they want with a baby? I'm not
ready to have a baby. How do they think we can
have sex like this? What if we don't have sex? What

is blood feeding? Am I going to become a vampire's whore? I can't bel—"

"Stop!" Jace commanded in his bouncer voice. It came in handy at the bar, like his power of persuasion carried through his vocal cords instead of his eyes. But it shouldn't. So, technically, he wasn't using it on his mate—even if it was to calm her the fuck down.

Cassie stopped in her tracks, her chest heaving like she'd been out for a run. The material of her shirt was dirty with faint blood stains from her hand, or his hand, which wouldn't stop seeping. Whatever the metal was that made the oozing wound wasn't silver, but the wound refused to mend.

She remained still, finally looking directly at him. She looked just as gorgeous now as she did when he picked her up last night. Her rumpled, gauzy shirt hinting at the curves that lay underneath, the capris complementing her world-class runner's legs, her sandals—amazingly still on by those leather straps he'd love to snap with his fangs, displaying polished toes he'd imagined himself nibbling on.

Shiiiit. Her scent was overwhelming the small structure. X was right, he normally was half-mast around Cassie, but this was… intense. He was hard and throbbing, and it hurt so good. She must be in equal discomfort—hot and needy, wanting only release after release. What would it feel like to slide into her slick furnace as she wrapped her legs around him, clutching his ass, pulling him in deeper—

"You're eyes are glowing," her voice shook.

What a shitbag he was. They weren't shut in here even five minutes and he was imagining his pleasure over her pain.

Cassie moved to pace again, but he cut her off. "I want to talk, Cassie, but you need to trust me to be close to you. We can both resist."

"And if we can't resist—"

"Cassie. *Trust me.*"

Her cocoa eyes searched his, determining the sensibility of his words. She crossed her arms around her middle. "I *burn.*"

"I know, Tinkerbell. I'm sorry." Jace eased toward her, and when she didn't dart away, he wrapped his arms around her. Fuck, she was on fire. It was the first time he was able to just hold her since he'd met her. What he wouldn't give for it to be under different circumstances.

Cassie melted into him, seeking emotional comfort from his embrace. Soon she would be seeking physical comfort, and in a cruel twist of fate after months of waiting for her, weeks of chasing her, when she came begging to him, he was somehow going to have to resist until they escaped.

"Does it bother you?" she asked. "Being kept in this tiny room?"

"'Cuz it's the size of a prison cell?" he chuckled softly. "No, there's so much more that bothers me about this than another tiny cell." Jace leaned down to speak directly in her ear. "And besides, unlike prison, this place we may actually be able to escape."

Wide, questioning eyes met his as her body moved tighter against his. He didn't know if she realized it, but she'd started a steady rocking into him. Every fraction of excess pressure hardening his cock more. Maybe they could escape... if he had any blood cells left to power his brain when the time came.

"Let's move to the bed, so we can talk easier." When she stiffened, he added, "So you can lay next to me instead of rubbing up on me."

Her flushed face reddened further and she almost jumped the short distance to the bed. She lifted the sorry excuse for a blanket and inspected the sheet before deciding to crawl on. He joined her, both on their sides facing each other.

"How are we going to escape?" She hissed in a pain-laced voice, her legs were slowly scissoring against each other, trying to find some relief to the mounting pressure begging to be released.

"I don't have an exact plan."

The crestfallen look she gave him spoke volumes.

"There are more chances here than we had before," he tried to reassure her. "The Agents hate each other, the snipers I sensed were only human, they expect me to use my telepathic power, but to my knowledge they don't know how well I can fight. They'll expect me to fight four-legged, but I'm better on two and they won't be ready."

"So we wait."

He nodded. They lay in silence beside each other, waiting. Her squirming worsened, her hands inching their way down to her crotch, then she'd snap them back up.

"Tell me something bad. Something that will keep me from crawling on top of you. Talk about Sigma."

Keeping his arms folded in on himself, helpless to watch her struggle but knowing his touch would make it worse, he tried to resist drowning himself in the waves of delectable pheromones rolling off her, clouding the room. She was right. Talking about Sigma would put a slight damper on his mood.

"I don't know specifics, really. Maybe I would've if my family stayed with the pack, but I lived more human than wolf until the last few years. They were the bogeyman when I was little. An afterthought as I was growing up. Then at the club I heard things, watched for things. It's clear now they're well-funded, highly organized, increasingly trained, and there's rumors it might all be by vampires."

"Why?" Cassie curled into a loose ball, her hands clenched in between cramped thighs, rocking gently.

Talking about Sigma wasn't going to help lessen her urges, but she needed to be educated. He kept on, trying not get distracted at the exhilarating thought of watching his mate get herself off.

"You can't conquer the world from sundown to sunup without the aid of another species that can tolerate daylight. The great battle between shifters and vampires revolves around stopping bloodsuckers from trying to take over the world. They want to establish their own brand of feed lots, with shifters comprising the prime herd, and humans the chattel and slave labor."

"Why the prime herd?" Cassie managed the question between whimpers. Jace was beginning to doubt waiting it out until someone checked on them. Her desperation was getting to be too much for her and too much suffering for him to watch his mate go through, even if it was to save them both... and a yet unmade baby. No, he wouldn't fuck for them; they wouldn't get his mate or any of his future progeny.

"If a vampire drains a shifter, it can acquire our strengths and our abilities. It could tolerate sun for a short period of time, it could use our mental capabilities temporarily. Then we'd heal, and they'd drain us again."

"It?" More moaning, then some shuttering breaths. "What do vampires look like?"

Ugly fuckers, Jace wanted to say. How did he explain without disturbing her further, that they were stunning? Beautiful. Creatures of the night that hunted humans with their minds and bodies. "They look like you'd want them to suck your blood."

"Great. Hot vampires. Awesome," Cassie ground out between moans. "I really need the Guardians to come with me to talk to that patient I had committed. I really thought he lost it, but I think everything he was saying was true."

Tears ran down her face. "Jace… I can't do this. It hurts so bad. What do we do?"

His mind raced for answers. "Let me ease you. We can give them a show. We've got a blanket for cover, we can make it look and sound like we're having sex when I'm just giving you some release."

He expected resistance, some sort of excuse from his rational female who never acted on impulse. Instead, she flipped the blanket over them and frantically unbuttoned her pants. Before he could tell her to slow down, she grabbed his hand bringing it into the furnace of her feminine folds.

The breath whooshed out of him. *Fuuuuck*, she was on fire. The bed should be smoldering under her delicate body. Still holding his wrist with both hands, she fervently rocked against him. Jace clenched his jaw so hard his teeth might break. He didn't move otherwise. Didn't kiss her, didn't wrap her up in his embrace, didn't even twine his legs through hers—not that he could, they were securely clenched.

His mate fell apart against his hand within seconds, the strength of her orgasm slamming against his mental shields, urging him to finish joining their bodies. For a brief moment she lay still, sweat beading her forehead, eyes closed, her breathing slowing for the first time since the drugs hit.

"How do we stop this?" Cassie pondered, eyes still closed. The fire burning within her temporarily cooled, but the insidious burn began again where his hand was still joined with her body. "I want my body back. I want that sick feeling in my chest to go away."

Sick feeling? Was the dose effecting her whole body? Or did she mean their connection, the place in her heart where she could feel him and know he was hers? They were forever linked, two joined as one. Did she want to break that link? The very thought devastated him.

"*Jaaaace.*" Her hands released their clasp on his wrist to grab his shirt collar and press herself closer to him.

"I'll help you as much as you need, baby. Just like this. If I do more—kiss you, hold you, see any bare inch of your lovely body—I don't think I can stop. Your scent is calling to me, driving me crazy, making my wolf want to howl sensing your need." With that he rolled her over onto her back, and rose above her, his fingers deftly working her fevered flesh. She was soaked, her juices coating him and her panties as she rode his hand. He longed to be down there, using his tongue instead to lap at her sweet release before taking her with the part of the his body that was in extreme pain, straining against his jeans to get to her, continuing to thicken with each wave of his female's desire.

He slid one finger into her tight channel. Cassie bucked, clenching around him so he couldn't slide a second one in. Grinding his teeth together, thinking of only her comfort and ignoring his own raging need keeping him as solid as granite, he leaned his head down next to hers, in case he did something detrimental to this situation and kiss her, because it wouldn't stop at a kiss. He concentrated only on his fingers, working them in and out of her taut body, and not on how the creamy tops of her breasts peeked from her shirt. Rejecting how easy it would be to lift the hem up and expose her flushed skin so he could cool her off by licking paths along her torso and blowing on them. Yeah, he had to disregard all that.

She fisted his shirt, twisting, almost tearing it off as her second orgasm slammed through her. Her jean-clad legs spread far apart underneath him, wrapped around his waist briefly, before falling limp to the rumpled sheet. With her eyes closed again, utilizing this moment of reprieve to finally relax from the tension coursing through her splendid body, her head lolled to the side and she appeared like she could drift off into an easy sleep.

"You're beautiful," he couldn't help but murmur in her ear.

"You're full of shit," she murmured back. Turning her head and opening her eyes, their faces an inch apart, she said, "This isn't right."

"We'll make it work," he reassured her. They were forcefully mated, but he was confident that he could've won her over, gained her acceptance so it would've been inevitable. They were still together, he'd continue to be patient until she felt comfortable with their joining.

"No," Cassie shook her head. "We've got to get it out of me."

Confused, he didn't have time to ponder what she meant. She abruptly pushed him back, sliding out from under him. She retched as she hit the floor and dove for the bucket in the corner. Cassie curled over it, gagging and heaving, her body trembling.

Her sudden illness tamped down his raging desire. She lost what was left of their supper and the dessert they'd shared last night. Soon she'd be out of undigested products and her heaving showed no signs of letting up. Massaging her shoulders, he kept telling her she'd be okay, he'd make sure of it.

In between retches, she gasped, "I can't keep doing this. It won't stop. What did they give me?"

Grimly, he said, "I don't know. Maybe they didn't account for any interactions with other meds you're taking. Are you on the pill?" He didn't scent her fertility at any point they were together so he suspected she was taking something to stop it. Female shifters didn't need to as they only became fertile with their mates, and then it was cyclic after that with long periods in between. They lived a long time; there was no need to yield to a monthly need to procreate. The theory was that human mates continued their normal cycles since it was more difficult to create interspecies young.

Another round of dry heaves. His ears just caught her answer of "shot" in between. Sigma fucked up something they gave her. The drugs were intended to keep her writhing on the bed until he gave in to palliate them both. If they were going to keep her like this instead, she wouldn't survive the rest of the day. Despite the waves of pheromones rolling off her, he didn't sense fertility from her. Either it was too soon, or the drugs weren't working like Sigma thought they should.

Cassie sat back on her knees, wiping her mouth weakly with the back of her hand. Jace remained behind her, rubbing her back. There was no bathroom, no sink in this hut. To Madame G, they were just rutting animals ruled by instinct and hormones.

"God, I still burn," she croaked, squirming. But the movement set off another tidal wave of pheromones and again the intended response did not occur, instead she bent back over the bucket retching noisily.

Cassie continued for a few more rounds, while Jace pounded on the door yelling that his mate was sick. After one intense episode, he abandoned the door to kneel beside her again. She pushed away the bucket and remained on her hands and knees, attempting to crawl away.

"Do you want to be back on the bed? Let me carry you." He reached around her to help her up and she fell limp in his arms.

* * *

Splintering wood drew Cassie back to consciousness. This structure might be enhanced like the Agents, but it wasn't going to hold up to a male terrified for his mate. The building shook again as Jace rammed the weakening door with his body. Voices shouted outside, the Agents preparing to take him down as soon as he stepped into daylight. They could kill him.

No! Her voice didn't work.

One last mighty kick from his heavily-booted foot rendered the door useless. A strip of wood still hung where the deadbolts and doorknobs remained, the rest of the door ripped from the hinges.

"I'm bringing her out," Jace called. "Don't fucking shoot. She's sick."

"Did I or did I not say that this was a shit plan and he'd tear this place apart with his bare hands, hmmm?" X was out in the trees with them, still as convivial as ever. "Relax big guy. Grab your girl and we'll take her to our lovely abode, get her back in working order."

Cassie weakly struggled into a sitting position as Jace stalked toward her, concern and determination on his handsome features. She shook her head. "No, no, no. We can't go with them."

Gathering her in his arms, he brought his mouth close to ear so he could speak without being overheard. "We'll make our move soon, but we've got to get you out of here."

Maneuvering them through the remnants of the door, Jace stepped outside. Cassie blinked rapidly against the strength of the sun but Jace didn't flinch or squint in the slightest. His diamond gaze swept the Agents in front of him and the surrounding woods, inhaling to determine scents and locations.

"Car's here," X announced, as Cassie heard the crunching of tires in the distance. They must've set this up near a remote road so they didn't have far to drag two unconscious bodies in the dark last night. "Remember… you're still in our crosshairs…" X finished in a sing-song voice, crossing in front of them to meet the on-coming SUV.

The vehicle bumped along the unkempt gravel road where grasses and weeds had grown into the wheel tracks. A man, all in camouflage like the others, drove and Agent D was in the passenger side. Both men climbed out after pulling to a stop. The driver, holding a long-range rifle, opened the back door, expecting Cassie and Jace to get inside. If they got into that backseat, it was over. They would have no more chances to escape, they would be Madame G's toys, her baby-making factory at whim.

Agent D covered the other side. The ornate dagger box was still hooked to his belt. Why it needed to be kept in their vicinity, she didn't know, but she did know that if she could get a hold of it, she'd have their key to freedom from the oily clutches of the dark lady and her devoted Agents. Even in her sickened state, she could feel the tight clench of evil around her heart tightening with the dagger so close.

Jace held onto Cassie as tightly as he could, tensed and ready to spring. Cassie wondered what he sensed that she couldn't. She wrapped her arms around him as best she could, her injured hand still slowly oozing from Madame G's dagger. Her stomach roiled with each movement, but the shot of adrenaline from breaking free of the cabin and the uncertainty of their escape kept her hormones from skyrocketing further and making her sick all over Jace.

The wind kicked up, rustling old leaves, and died down just as quickly. For a moment, it was eerily silent, and then Cassie heard it—howling. More than one wolf bayed in the distance and they were closing in.

"And there they are," X muttered.

"Guardians," the driver confirmed. "Get in." he ordered.

That was the last thing Cassie wanted to do, but she understood why Jace finally acquiesced. Left outside, it was at least three to two, if she would even be counted as an opponent in her weakened condition. She had no idea how many Agents were still in the woods, and the steel around the vehicle would provide some protection if gunfire were to break out.

Jace set her gently inside and was sliding in next to her when she heard the muffled gunshot and shouts from the woods. He immediately covered her with his body as the driver slammed the door behind him. They were left alone in the SUV while the Agents attempted to standoff against the Guardians.

"You okay?" Jace asked.

Cassie nodded, as much as she could with her head tucked under his protective upper body.

"The Guardians just took out a sniper, and I think they got them both. Cassie, do you think you can run? At all?"

Cassie nodded again, her stomach lurching at the thought, but it wouldn't matter. She'd throw up on the go if she had to.

"We're surrounded by the Guardians. As soon as there's an opening between the three Agents left, we're gone. Understand?"

Cassie peeked up, out of Jace's embrace, to look out the window. The remaining, and most formidable Agents had them surrounded. X and the driver with his rifle were on one side, with Agent D still on the passenger side, but all three faced the trees where the Guardians prowled.

"Don't lose that dagger, Double D," X called over her shoulder, checking on the couple. "We wouldn't want to nullify this whole deal."

"Shut the fuck up X!" Agent D angrily shouted back at her.

"Do you have sights on them?" the driver shouted.

"Negative," X replied calmly, gun in one hand, whipping around when the SUV rocked slightly with the sound of hissing air. "Fuck, they got a tire. We'll need to have a good old fashioned standoff."

Agent D unloaded the clip from one of his weapons into the trees, firing almost blindly. When he opened the vehicle door to dig out another clip from a metal chest in the front, he caught Cassie looking at the dagger box dangling from his belt.

"Face down, you dog-humping bitch," he snarled, shoving the fresh clip in, the waves of hate for them rolling off him. She jerked her head back down. He must've been an easy recruit for Madame G.

Jace coiled over her, a low growl rumbling from his chest. "You already had your warning... *Double D*," he stressed snidely. Cassie drew in on herself, knowing Agent D wouldn't allow an insult from Jace pass.

The comment earned a snarl from the man leaning across the front seat and he lunged toward Jace to slam the butt of his gun into Jace's skull. Before Cassie could draw in a breath to warn Jace, he reached over with a speed she didn't know he possessed, grabbed Agent D's hand on the gun, and slammed his arm straight over the seat. Bones crunched and the gun dropped into her lap. Agent D cried out in pain, drawing a knife with his other hand to strike at Jace's throat.

Cassie flung her hand up to send it off its intended path. The knife ripped across the fabric of the SUV's ceiling. Jace grabbed the gun from her lap, reached back, and shoved it into Agent D's chest pulling the trigger.

Cassie yelped, Agent D slumped over, and all that could be heard was her own and Jace's heavy breathing. The Sigma Agents had to have heard the shot. Would they come rushing back to the vehicle and deal with them, or did the shot get lost in the ones already being traded between the Agents and the Guardians?

The wolves were baying, closer this time, but so random and frequently it was hard to tell how far away and how many there were. The Agents outside the car fired shots into the woods, those shots getting returned by tufts of dirt and leaves flying up around the Agents' feet.

Jace rummaged through Agent D's pockets for more weapons while Cassie snagged the dagger box.

"It's time to run. If we can get into the woods, we have a chance." Jace eased the back passenger door open for them to drop out since the death of Agent D left the much sought after opening they needed.

"Is he dead?" It made her feel better to whisper. She didn't know if it was necessary but all of these people heard way better than Cassie.

"I don't sense a heartbeat, but they said he was enhanced so…" Jace helped her glide down to the ground, still clutching the opulent box to her chest, scarcely making any noise on the rough gravel. He moved down next to her with a grace and assuredness that made up for his size.

What does that mean? She didn't want to hang around Agent D in case "hopefully dead" didn't mean well and truly dead. Not willing to make any more commotion, even with just a whisper, she remained silent, waiting for Jace's instruction.

Afraid any movement would make a sound, she looked questioningly at him. His brows were drawn together as he scanned the woods to determine their best route. They had to get to cover fast, otherwise the remaining two Agents could easily wound them, or worse. They weren't distracted enough to not see or hear them trying to get away.

Cassie almost missed the wolf, it barely moved, waiting in the thicker foliage of the trees, completely camouflaged. Jace rose, taking her with him, and used his body to shield her from the driver and X as they took off into the same dark area the wolf appeared from.

X and the driver shouted. Sheer terror spurred her forward. She was a moving target with a giant bulls-eye printed on her back. Wood chips exploded from trees around her as bullets made their mark. She was sure she would lose Jace, be unable to keep up since he effortlessly kept pace with her frantic fleeing through the trees.

More gunfire echoed through the trees. Cassie stole a glance over her shoulder. The two remaining Agents were being held off by gunfire from the woods.

Her foot caught on a tree root and she dropped the box, flying headfirst next to a tree trunk. Jace's strong arms lifted her back up so they could keep running.

"Wait the box!" she cried. Jace found it first, tucked it into his side, and grabbed her hand with his free one. Their pace was no longer the initial frantic run to get away as fast as possible, but more of a quick rush allowing her to pick through the brush with relative ease.

Slaps from low-hanging branches stung her face and her sliced hand burned, but it could have been much worse.

Cassie drew in a quick breath as a wolf veered in running next to them. She hoped the beast was a Guardian.

The terrain became steep and Jace had to let her go so they could clamber up using all fours. A dark form waited at the top. Cassie could make out the outline of a wolf. But which one?

Jace dropped behind her to help finish their ascent, and with his hand on her back guided her over. "Stop here," and they dropped down to their bellies.

"What's the plan, boss?" Jace spoke quietly, peering up and over to get a view of where they'd come from.

Boss? Wasn't that—? Cassie yelped as she looked up to find a very naked Christian standing there. She looked away, knowing she was blushing furiously, and it shouldn't matter; they were running for their lives. The random naked men, she'd never get used to.

"The Guardians are holding off X and E, but without the firepower they can only do so much. Kaitlyn's got the long-range weapon, and one of the twins is on his way with more firepower, but we didn't have much time to mobilize when I got your call."

"Kaitlyn's out here?" Cassie's concern for her friend added to the concern for herself and Jace.

"Helluva shot she is, too. Which is good for us."

"We keep heading toward town, then." Jace stated more than questioned.

Christian nodded. "Keep following me, we stay ahead of them we're good, but…" He shook his head and looked out, his predator eyes reflecting silvery green. "Even if X doesn't turn, we've got to move. She can still fly faster than a motherfucker and that E isn't a vamp, but he ain't normal, either. They both can haul it."

"E's the driver, then? The Guardians won't take them on?" Jace asked, scanning the area, his eyes reflecting like his boss's.

Christian shook his head. "Commander Fitzsimmons wants X taken alive, but her and E are too good, been partners too long. They can hold off several Guardians and cause major trauma." Christian rolled his massive shoulders, moved his head side-to-side, stooping. "Besides, they don't want to kill you and we need to know why."

He dropped to all fours and his skin transformed into dark fur as he flowed into the form of a large wolf in seconds.

Cassie looked into Jace's now silver hologram eyes. "If you shift, you can move faster."

"I'm no good to you out here naked on all fours." He leaned in and planted a quick kiss on her.

She closed her eyes briefly, wanting to enjoy the sensation, but feeling as if there was a vice squeezing her around her ribs. "It's not right. This mating."

His face was grim. "No, it wasn't." He grabbed her hand and gave it a reassuring squeeze. "We'll work it out when we get back. We'll be good." And he started moving forward, picking up the pace, the dark box still tucked into his side.

"But it's not right," she repeated, wishing they could stop and talk all this out. That's what she did. She talked things out—with herself, with her patients, with Dad... But this feeling of wrongness that settled deep into her after the ceremony would take more than a quick peck and a few words of reassurance to repair what was really wrong. Their flight for freedom, and burning through much of the hormonal overload from the drugs, left the vice of evil around her chest a prominent feeling.

They were making their way through the woods at a decent pace, but Cassie knew it wasn't enough. She'd run five days a week for over ten years, but she could not compete against supernatural creatures born to rule the woods. Nor could she compete against enhanced humans who were probably enhanced to hunt supernatural creatures in dark woods.

Her hand slipped out of Jace's, both of their hands not healing well from the ceremony, and she went down with an *umph*. Jace bent to help her up. "We're almost to Christian's car. The main road's close."

Cassie couldn't tell if he was lying to make her feel better and give her courage to keep going. Weeks spent camping with her father had given her an appreciation for the outdoors as he'd taught her how to navigate the land. It wasn't enough under the circumstances. "Sorry to slow you down."

She saw a flash of teeth as he shot her a quick grin. "You're actually doing pretty well. I'm even having a hard time on two legs."

"Yeah, well," she got out between breaths as they rushed on, "my dad was big on survival shit. You know, scared the government was after us and all so he took us 'off the grid' as he called it."

Jace turned and gave her a confused look. "The government was after your dad?"

She shook her head to save a breath. "He only thought so. After mom died, he quit taking his meds, he had schizophrenia. Lived in paranoia and took me with."

"How'd it end?"

"Troopers found our car we'd been living out of by the river. Took us in. He went to inpatient psych and I went to Kaitlyn's."

"I'm sorry."

If they weren't running, she would've shrugged. "Mom's passing devastated him. They lived for each other. I don't hold going crazy against him."

Jace grew quiet, she knew what he was thinking. This whole mating, binding their souls together, was outside of her comfort zone for a good reason. Tie herself eternally to someone who became her everything so she could lose her ever-loving mind if he died before her? Oh wait, her life force would be bound to his. So if he went before her, good-bye Cassie. Would she do that for him? Maybe. If they figured out this disgusting mating ritual that made her hand continuously burn and her insides feel slimy. *This isn't right.*

They continued moving as quickly through the terrain as they could, dodging branches and remaining upright. Christian was up ahead, guiding them, but Cassie couldn't see him, instead relying on Jace's supernatural sense to pick up where the large, black wolf was. The howling in the distance was getting closer, the Guardians could only hold off the two Agents for so long against gunfire.

So Alex—X—had been watching her, studying her. Enough that she knew when Cassie ran and where. Cassie wasn't stupid, she took different routes and wasn't routine about her times. Those weeks without Jace, she ran a lot and if it was at the same time, it wasn't the same place. That wasn't her daddy's paranoia shining through, it was simple street smarts.

But Sigma still found her, knew she was a shifter's mate, knew where to find her, and when both of them were together. No one in her personal or professional life knew about Jace except Kaitlyn. Pale Moonlight. If it was a known hangout of shifters, then it would make sense mates could be found there, too. *But why?*

"Why us Jace?" she asked quietly, not needing to speak up with his sensitive ears. "Why did they come after us?"

She glanced over at him, his face grim.

"They're all about opportunity, Tinkerbell. They must've recognized what I am and my interest in only you." That part set a smug glow warming its way through her. Take that, khaki and cardigan wearing naysayers. "As for forcing us to mate and watch…" The warm glow was gone, replaced by cold dread. "I can only guess," he hesitated, "they thought you being human would be easier to capture. And humans have more fertile cycles, although it tends to be harder for them to reproduce."

Two shots sounded closer, Cassie jumped, a wolf yelped. Jace gripped her hand harder, tugging her along even faster. From up ahead, Christian gave two sharp barks.

"We're almost there," Jace assured her.

Cassie thought she saw a lighter clearing up ahead, must be the road. Jace pulled her up over an incline where she could see the car, and a very naked Christian pulling up his pants. They raced toward him through the ditch down to the clearing. Cassie saw puffs of gravel pop up beside the car.

"Fuck! They caught up." In one smooth move, Jace shoved the box into Cassie's arms and swung her up into his arms so her vitals were protected by his body. Frantically, she tried to hold on to the box while being bounced against his hard chest. She was unable to wrap an arm around him.

"We need the Agents to undo this. To unmate us," Cassie looked up from his arms.

He frowned, looking down at her. "It'll be all right. We'll get to safety and talk. I'll take care of you."

No, no, no, she shook her head. "It's not *right*," she stressed.

"It will be. Don't worry." He ran straight to the car and opened the door to set her in. Christian was mostly dressed now, standing with the driver's door open, holding his own weapon toward the woods they came out of, covering them. She slid down, but didn't sit, Jace turned, his back to her. The gun he'd taken from Agent D trained on the tree line.

"Commander," an unseen X called in a sing-song voice from the woods. Cassie couldn't make out where she was, but E must have been close, too, unless the wolves got him. The wolves were silent, stalking. "I wouldn't try that," she laughed. "My partner has his sights on you."

X slowly stepped out from the edge of the woods onto the high rise above the road, her green eyes developing a faint glow.

"And I've got my sights on the newly-mated, here," she finished, looking down her barrel toward Jace.

Half of Cassie wanted to freeze in terror, crawl into the backseat face down and let the wolves rescue her. The other half, wanted to do something, anything, that would help.

Seconds ticked by, but the standoff held. There was no way out of this without someone dying. Jace would die protecting her. The Guardians would die protecting her and their species. Christian would die protecting his pack, which she was now part of.

Jace raised his arms higher, his aim directly on X. "Don't come any closer."

"Oh, but you see, Boo," X purred, "you're nice and newly mated. And even better, to a human. So you see, I need you. I'd hate to hurt you, but you'll heal. She might not if we take this to the next level."

Another beat of silence.

"No offense, Baby Boo," X's vibrant green gaze flicked to Cassie, "I wouldn't be after your man if he wasn't attached to you."

Cassie's gaze was captivated by X's strong pull. Something X said earlier rang through her mind. *We wouldn't want that thing to plunge into one their hearts.* Did she really say that earlier?

X darted behind a tree as bark flew off exactly where her face had been. Snarls and growls in the distance suggested that E was taking on one of the Guardians while shots were exchanged between the edge of the woods and the car. Jace and Christian kept X from advancing.

"Get in the car, Cassie!" Jace pumped off shots slower than his boss to save ammo.

Cassie quickly turned and dropped the box onto the seat, fumbling with the clasps. X's voice continuing to burn in her mind, *Nullify this whole deal…*

Her hands shaking, she gripped the handle with both hands knowing she'd have to shove hard and fast for this to work.

Jace peeked over his shoulder. "Get in!"

Trembling from head to toe with what she was about to do, but knowing with no uncertainty this was exactly what she had to do. She raised the dagger up, gathered all her strength, and plunged.

"Stop her!" X ordered.

Praying her aim was true, the blade slid into the middle of Jace's back, through his ribs, into his heart. Searing pain tore through Cassie's side.

As if in slow motion, Jace's arms fell to his sides, he dropped to his knees, toppling face-first into the gravel.

"Jace?" Christian barreled around the front of the car. X had disappeared, there was no more gunfire. Wolves in half transition came sprinting from the trees—Commander Fitzsimmons and Bennett.

Cassie pressed her hand to her side, the pain increasing. Wet. Warm. She stared dumbly at her bloody hand, at her torso covered in red, at Jace, lying face-down on the road. Then… complete darkness.

Chapter Twelve

She'd ripped his fucking heart out. Literally. He sat there, in the stark white hospital room that was kept way too warm. Cassie's form covered in drab white blankets, a sterile odor perfuming the air. It'd been three days. Three days of watching, at first with machines breathing for her, at nurses and aids coming and going, at Cassie not move. She was finally breathing on her own now, but still unconscious.

He shouldn't be here at all. He'd give her the freedom she wanted from him. Fucking Guardians. They talked him into this. No, not the bedside vigil. That, he couldn't help himself. He'd leave when she regained even a semi-conscious state. No, they needed his power. It got tricky bringing a human with a gunshot wound into a hospital and not being able to explain how a secret agency was after supernatural beings and Cassie got shot stabbing him in the heart. Doctors and police don't take "I don't know, it just happened" as much of an explanation.

For the last three days, he stared so many people in the eyes convincing them it was a misfire—some poacher out in the woods when she was out for a run, no need to look further, it'd do no good. Whoever it was was long gone. It was almost harder to convince some of the hospital staff that he could hang out in her room, looking as haggard and heartbroken as he did.

That night they were nabbed was pure hell—the worry about Cassie, meeting the infamous Madame G, getting caught between Guardian and Sigma crossfire. But for a brief couple of hours, he'd felt whole. Like all that waiting, watching her and being patient, paid off. She was his. They'd get out from Madame G's clutches, do up the ceremony right so they had something sweet to remember, instead of something from a horror movie. Then get down to the mating basics.

When he came to the next morning, after they'd pulled the dagger from his heart, he'd felt empty. So completely empty. He suspected before Christian told him what had happened. Feeling manipulated by him after what X revealed, she must have begun to despise him, and was desperate enough to not be bound to him, she was willing to try to kill him.

Initially, he refused to come down to the hospital. The human docs would take care of her, she'd be fine. He'd be fine. That was a lie, but if he told it enough, he'd start to believe it. *Fucking Guardians*. Fucking Bennett starting in about protecting their race and needing Jace's special form of persuasion. Trying to convince him it'd be like the other times they utilized Jace's skills. It wasn't. This woman, who was his everything, had become his only family, hadn't been lying near death those other times. He couldn't stay away. But he would move on. She didn't want him.

Dawn was approaching. His keen ears heard the docs on their rounds mention that she was making progress and should be coming around soon, and if all went well by tomorrow, Cassie would be moved. They anticipated a quick recovery; she was young and healthy. No major damage had been done, the units of blood they gave her after surgery doing their job.

He'd go back to the club. Do the books, maybe bartend a little. Commander Fitzsimmons offered him a spot on the team. He wasn't a born Guardian, but Sigma's network had become encompassing, advanced, and multi-dimensional. The Guardians already used his talents on several occasions, but they could use the rest of his mind and body. Someone who could go out and do field work, then come back and keep their finances in order and growing, the commander had said. The Guardians needed to start adapting to match their foes: advance their technology, learn about the experiments being carried out on their species and why, and take control of their gifts.

The rumors were true. Most of the West Creek Guardians struggled with their mental gifts for unknown reasons, relying instead on blades, bullets, and brawn. It was the main reason they were dispatched to West Creek, their lack of finesse would be an advantage dealing with the pack on the wrong side of the tracks, or river in this case. Master Bellamy was confident that he could work with Jace, that his gift may not be dependent on eye contact, but could also influence through his voice like when he calmed Cassie down in the shack. Since Jace appeared to have a good mastery of his skill all the times he'd used it, Master Bellamy was confident they could build Jace's mental strength and dexterity wielding it.

Jace exhaled and rubbed his face, his decision made.

A deep sigh came from the bed. His gaze flicked up. Her head was turned away, but her eyelids fluttered. That was his cue and he was gone.

***

He wasn't answering her calls. She'd tried every day. She woke up feeling his presence and then, nothing. He was gone. When she was released two days later, her dad had brought her home. He was her only emergency contact, even though they hadn't had much contact over the last fifteen years.

Her dad who'd been staying with her to care for her was worried. At least that made one man in her life. She called into work, needing a few weeks of medical leave to recover and wanting some time off to regain a foothold on her life. And to track down Jace.

Why wasn't he answering? She hit the end button, not nearly as satisfying as slamming a good old-fashioned phone down.

"You gonna tell me anything yet?"

She looked at her dad, the concern spread across his face, wishing she could unload the last few weeks on him, but refusing to risk setting him back mentally. *Get this, Dad. There really is a secret agency and they were after me.* He'd been stable for years, after his long stint in the mental health ward. She kept him at arm's length, admittedly feeling guilty for not helping him more, for turning him in to authorities. Her grown-up self would claim she had been just a kid and her dad needed help. That little girl who missed the time with her dad, hunting and fishing, trekking through the wilderness, bonding over missing her mother would disagree. She could have lied to the trooper who found them in the woods that day. Could've said they were fine, instead of the truth that led to tearing them apart for so many years.

Gray Stockwell looked at her with fatherly love, never having held a grudge against his only child for both saving herself and distancing herself from him. "You can talk to me, you know. I won't break."

Maybe she should talk to him. Give him an edited version, for sure. She last spoke to him when she was cancelling wedding plans. He asked what happened. All she said was Grant dumped her. End of story. Only it was the beginning.

With a sigh, she put her phone down. "I met a man after Grant and I broke things off." That sounded good. A little better than *I went out to get smashed after I was dumped and brought a strange man home that same night*. That's not a line to tell her dad, no matter what the rest of the story was.

Gray remained silent, waiting for her to continue. Her mind whirred at how to phrase the rest of the story.

"I tried not to get serious fast. He was patient with me. He's liked me for a long time. Then I fell for him—hard—but I think he thinks I betrayed him."

"And he's avoiding your calls?"

Cassie swallowed hard and nodded, pacing her living room. Not usually a crier, tears burned the back of her eyes. Home for three days, she needed rest, but tried to be up and moving more and more each day. When she got off the pain meds, she would hunt that frustrating, big, bald man down. Fantasies of being strong enough to slam into Pale Moonlight, like a scene from an old western, demanding to talk to her man, kept the pain at bay so she could work on getting strong again.

"Was he the big man who kept a bedside vigil when I couldn't be there?"

Cassie stopped and stared at her dad. The gray at his temples, peppering through his hair, fit his name. "He was there?"

"Tall, shaved head?" She nodded. He kept going, a hint of humor in his eyes. "I only saw him once, but heard several nurses gushing about him and the other men who brought you in." He gave a pointed stare. "You've been hanging out with a different crowd lately."

"They're good men," she said defensively.

"And you're a good judge of character. And I'm glad. Everyone saw you and Grant weren't right together... except you and Grant." She raised her brows at her dad's bold statement. Gray usually tiptoed around her, kept conversation superficial to prevent bad memories from being dredged up. She realized how much she kept her father at arm's length, how much it hurt their relationship.

"So tell me more about this man." Gray settled back into the sofa.

The pain in her side reaching a dull roar, Cassie settled back into her recliner, her recovery area of choice, and told her dad all about Jace. As they talked, *really talked*, Cassie marveled over the growing relationship with her dad. It took getting shot for them to reach this point, to get her to move out of her own way and live life. Enjoy her dad being a dad and she accepted they were only human and he might go off-kilter again, but she'd be there. That night in the woods when she feared she might lose Jace forever, when he risked everything to save her, made her want to spend eternity with him. Their false bond had been destroyed, but her love for him was real. She dreamed of hanging onto him on the back of his motorcycle and riding into the sunset. After she had a chance to explain why she stabbed him in the heart.

Cassie's eyes got heavy, her energy spent. Her dad brought over a blanket as she drifted off.

"Rest up, Cassie. He'll be waiting for you… if he knows what's good for him."

***

"He's not here," Commander Fitzsimmons said.

She drove up to the compound, after being lost for an hour because the Guardians somehow erased her car's GPS. *Fucking Guardians*. A Guardian she'd never met her at the front door, ignored her inquiry regarding Jace, and got the commander.

She wasn't getting a warm reception anywhere. Stabbing their friend through the heart didn't endear her to anyone. Didn't they realize she had saved them all? Jace deserved her explanation and she would wait to talk to him first.

The club had been a dead end. Surprised to find the door open midmorning, she breezed inside. Christian had been standing behind the bar, leaning over a laptop, a pretty woman at his side. He straightened when he saw her and gave her no greeting other than a dark eyebrow lifting.

"I need to talk to him," was all Cassie said.

The woman straightened also, her dark eyes full of distain. As short as Christian was tall, this must be Mabel, his mate. She crossed her arms in front of her chest, eying Cassie up and down, the tight curls springing from her head bouncing from the movement. Refusing to shrivel under the obviously powerful woman's scrutiny, Cassie remained where she was, resisting the urge to fidget.

"He does not wish to talk with you. You may leave." Mabel's rich voice resonated through Cassie's bones, wanting to make her turn abruptly and leave.

"I'd like to hear that from him. Where is he?" Cassie demanded.

Mabel raised an eyebrow and shifted her stance. Christian's second eyebrow joined his already raised first one.

"He is not here. You may leave," Mabel said again.

Resisting the urge to turn and run out the door, she said first, "Tell him I need to talk to him."

It was well into the afternoon now as she found herself in the compound facing off with the imposing commander. She was tired, needed a pain pill, and was getting cranky.

"Do you know where he is?" she asked testily.

"No." Man of many words, that one.

She was tempted to turn and go. No one needed an explanation but Jace. Yet, something had been bugging her as she relived that night over and over.

"Commander, is X nothing but an evil Sigma Agent?"

The commander stilled even further, if that was possible. His intense hazel gaze drilled into her.

"Why?"

Mabel couldn't make her fidget, but the commander might. She felt as if her response would determine how she left their headquarters. What kind of history did he and the X have?

"I can read people well, even if they aren't human," she said. The commander's eyes narrowed. "We ran together a couple of times. Now I know she was playing me, setting me up. But in the woods, Agent D was psychotic in his hatred of us. X was aloof, almost. And it felt like she hinted how to get the curse off of us, even though it appeared she was baiting D."

"It wasn't a curse, you were mated." The commander narrowed his eyes at her.

Well, shit, that pissed him off. "No, whatever happened out there wasn't mating." She rushed on, before he kicked her out, too. "And during the final standoff, I heard X's voice in my head, supporting what she'd said earlier in the night."

"How do you mean?" He wanted clarification, though it was like he already knew the answer.

"It was different from remembering what was said. It's like I heard her voice, in my head, *reminding* me of what she said, only I think there was more information. Does that make sense?"

He gave a curt nod and scanned the surrounding woods.

"She's been an Agent for a long time," he finally said. "If she were to defy Madame G in any way, it would mean torture, and, *if* she was lucky, death. But she's still alive. I wouldn't read more into it. She plays games."

Oookay. She did what she came here to do. Jace wasn't here, she could feel it and decided to call off her search and head home.

The OxyContin she took before bed released her mind from the throbbing in her side to the possibility that Jace may have indeed been at the club and Mabel may have tried her own persuasive techniques on her. His bike wasn't out front, but Cassie didn't recall seeing it out front any other time. And Jace may not have used any special powers on her, but nothing could stop Christian or Mabel. She walked in earlier today determined to rip the place apart looking for him, only to turn tail and get the fuck out when Mabel told her to.

Maybe he took off, most likely he didn't. Last night before succumbing to the pain meds, she went into Dr. Stockwell mode, analyzing the situation. He showed nothing but supreme patience and restraint. So riding off in a cloud of dust, leaving not only her after his secret bedside vigil—which told a lot in itself—but leaving school and work wasn't like him. Both of those brought him a lot of pride and acceptance, both of which he hadn't felt since his teens. His concern in the hospital told her he still cared about her.

So, no, he wasn't gone and she would plow through Christian and his formidable mate and tear that motherfucking bar apart looking for her man. She had one stop to make before she continued her hunt for her mate in the morning.

First, a good night's sleep.

***

"He's here and you can either let him know I'm out here or I can search every inch of this place." Cassie stood in the club, in front of the bar, looking around to determine where to start her search. And purposely avoiding eye contact with Christian. She wasn't sure if they needed that for their various gifts to work, but that's how Jace explained his. And both X and Mabel were looking into her eyes when she felt like she was getting messages from them.

"If he wanted to talk to you, don't you think he'd have done so by now?"

"Not if he thought I wanted nothing to do with him." Cassie walked back and forth looking for any office doors. "Jace! Jace, get out here!" Fine, she'd stomp and yell and shout.

"Stabbing a guy in the heart gives a man that idea," Christian said, calmly watching her pace around. Thankfully, Mabel wasn't here. Cassie could work around Christian, but she doubted Mabel would allow her to make a scene, eye contact or not. "You're not mated with him anymore, so go, live your life and give Jace peace."

Seeing no office spaces beyond the dance floor and The Den, she squared off in front of Christian. "That wasn't mating. It was something dark and vile and twisted. As long as that madwoman had her talons in us, we would never be free. She would have used it to hunt us."

"What do you mean?"

Cassie spun around at the male voice, her heart stuttered.

Arms crossed, muscles bulging from his black t-shirt, strong legs encased in the same black jeans, Jace was wary. He looked good, as always. His jaw clenched, eyes direct, he stood and waited. Where he appeared from, she had no clue, didn't care as long as he was there.

"Didn't you feel it?" She was confused. How could they not understand how she saved them? She didn't want trophies or accolades. She wanted acceptance that she did the right thing.

He scowled. "Being mated? Yeah, I fucking felt it. It felt great. Amazing. I felt complete."

What? How could it have been so different for him?

"Jace…" She moved closer to him, only to stop when he shook his head and held up his hand. She rushed on before either one of the males kicked her out. "Didn't you feel the darkness? I thought my insides were covered in black slime. It felt… evil, like that woman who mated us. You heard X, she was only interested in us because we were mated and she was a part of it. I couldn't stab myself to break the bond or I'd die. You said yourself, as long as everything's still attached, you'll heal. I'm sorry I hurt you, but I had to do it. For us."

A furrow developed in between Jace's brow, but he remained silent.

"It wasn't right. I had faith that we would heal and be able to mate the traditional way."

Christian chuckled behind her. She turned to glare at him, but noticed a smile play along Jace's lips.

Jace cleared his throat, throwing a hard look Christian's way. "The 'traditional way' is to copulate in front of witnesses. But we haven't done that in centuries."

The meaning of that was sinking in when Jace moved toward her.

"Did you mean that?" he was earnest. "You still want to be with me? Even after everything that happened?"

"*Because* of everything that's happened, I want to be with you."

"Then why," his voice dropped low, dangerous, and he was towering over her, "do you smell like your ex?"

Maybe she should've been scared, instead she rolled her eyes. "Are you serious?" Her anger spiking, she put her hands on her hips, "I dropped off our honeymoon tickets with him. I couldn't get my money back so I gifted them to him," she paused long enough to stand as tall as she was able and get into his face, "aaaand his new fiancé, my friend Emma." He looked momentarily stunned, so she continued. "I gave him a hug and told him not to feel guilty. You know… since he didn't know he was influenced. I told him he did the right thing when he broke things off." Her anger rose another notch. "I would like to think you thought better of me than that. Just like I know you haven't been with other women. You might be pissed at me, but you," she poked him in the chest, "are," *poke* "still," *poke* "mine," *poke*.

He was watching her hand each time she poked him. He followed the movement when she put it back on her hip. Then slowly, so slowly, his eyes made their way up her formfitting shirt, lingered on her breasts, watching them as they rose and fell with her breath, then burned their way up to meet her eyes. The heat from his look seared her.

A slow, lazy grin spread across his face. Her breath hitched, he was devastating before he smiled, but when he smiled, she lost herself. He took another step closer; she had to crane her head back to maintain eye contact.

Instead of leaning down for a kiss, he grabbed her butt and lifted her up, careful of her side, to meet his lips for a kiss. She hooked her shoes behind his back and threw her arms around his neck. His tongue invaded her mouth, his taste divine. It felt like an eternity since she'd last tasted him. He hugged her even closer, their tongues dueling, not stopping even as Christian broke into a slow clap and low chuckle behind them. Cassie smiled into the kiss, not willing to stop, either. Let him watch.

Epilogue

Jace was grinning like a dumb motherfucker and he didn't care. He stood in a clearing behind Guardian headquarters, surrounded by his coworkers. Sunlight filtered through the newly budded trees, casting a soft glow on Cassie's creamy skin, scattering highlights over her hair.

She stood across from him, absolutely gorgeous. And all his. Dressed in a simple, elegant white dress she repeated her vows. As his pack leader, Christian presided over the ceremony having the power and authority to properly mate them. He worried whether she would offer her hand for this part of the ritual, but she did so without hesitation.

Her only concern about today was not being able to have her dad present. They couldn't tell another human and risk their people. Cassie was unwilling to risk her dad's mental health by making him wonder about other bits of reality after learning shifters and vampires were real, and possibly still hunting Cassie.

Commander Fitzsimmons and Master Bellamy interrogated both of them about that night. They determined that the mating ceremony Madame G used was intended for the study of mating and combining lifespans. The evil presence Cassie felt may have indeed been the dark woman herself. Why Cassie could feel it, but not Jace, was also unknown. The only logical conclusion any of them came up with was the simplest—because she was human. Madame G has been ramping up her experiments on shifters and vamps, trying to conquer both species. She recruited humans, mysteriously enhanced them, but has never to their knowledge dealt with mating them. So, while she can settle a part of herself into the mating bond undetected to the wolves, she couldn't remain undetected by the humans. Or at least not Cassie, who also experienced increased immunity, more than most humans, to Mabel's mental shoves. Maybe it was Cassie, maybe it was the human mate of a shifter.

Christian finished the ceremony, presenting them with their proper mating dagger—a beautifully simple knife, not nearly as audacious as the first mating dagger. Cassie was told the *gladdus* was unique for each couple, signifying the strength of their blood bond and lasting love. Humans did rings, shifters did weapons.

Kaitlyn whooped and threw her flowers in the air. Jace's buddy and fellow bartender clapped him on the back. Both friends were asked to stand next to the couple as their witnesses. Jace grabbed Cassie around the waist and lifted her for the sealing kiss, wishing they could get away together and soon. Instead, they were waiting before taking some time off, since she had just gone back to work after her medical leave. As long as she came home to him every night, he didn't care. He would continue to do books for Christian while training someone new, but eventually he would belong to the Guardians—both his brain to help with the books and body for fighting. Kaitlyn kept giving him shit since he'd have to do some form of their training, and she'd no longer be the newbie.

Joining the Guardians wasn't an easy decision, but he wanted to be more useful to his species than to just keep the club running smoothly. A life lived in obscurity, fading into the background, was his mother's wish, not his. Sigma went after his mate. His primary concern was keeping her safe, then keeping the shifters in and around West Creek safe. After all, his mom and sister were still out there, and maybe they'd want less to do with a Guardian for a son and brother, but he'd be damned if they became targets. He'd made a vow to destroy Sigma, and Madame G along with it.

Cassie was content to move to the lodge, into a cabin of their own, and was happier being closer to Kaitlyn. Okay, she was thrilled and he'd endure Kaitlyn's high-pitched shriek of delight at the news all over again to make Cassie happy.

"Mr. Doctor Stockwell!" Bennett boomed, Cassie laughed. "Where's the free beer?"

Bennett was still attending therapy sessions with Cassie and agreed to go with her to interview her committed patient after the mating ceremony was completed. Cassie had gone back to her notes about the day she had him committed and brought what he'd said during his ravings to the commander. If there were any truth to them, Sigma's threat was greater than previously thought. Maybe he could give the Guardians information on the specific reasons behind Sigma's experiments.

A few of Christian's pack had asked about her job. Mental health services had never been an option for shifters before. Historically, they fought it out, but modern times and millions of cell phones with video was making that more difficult. That, along with the uniqueness of the troubled souls drawn to West Creek seeking Christian's authority, brought much interest in Cassie and her profession.

"Yeah, man. You promised us beer. Otherwise, I could sit at home and clean guns," Mercury chimed in, and probably wasn't joking. He'd been loosening up more around the group. Bennett was worried about him, since he didn't blow off steam at the club like he did with Mercury now that he was working with Cassie. Without Bennett to deal with any social interactions, Mercury quit going, too. With Kaitlyn around to needle him to try to get him to lighten up, or take out his excess aggression in the gym, he hadn't regressed.

Mercury had started running with Cassie on the woodland trails to watch out for her when Jace was training. Said he felt guilty "cuz your human almost died when we blew her off before." Jace was afraid she'd chafe under the extra security, but she said with Agents out there, she couldn't afford to be headstrong. Besides, Jace knew she seldom saw Mercury when he shadowed her, and when he did chat with her, she found his unwitting bluntness refreshing.

"Meet down at the club in an hour. Give the newly-mated time to consummate," Christian said. He winked at the happy couple. Jace's gaze devoured Cassie while a pretty stain touched her cheeks. "I closed it for the night. It can finally serve one of the main purposes it's meant for—a gathering spot for our pack and its Guardians for celebration and revelry." His former boss and pack leader looked out, his dark eyes taking in the small group of club employees—all part of his pack and the Guardians, before finally settling on his mate.

Mabel turned to the group and in her soft, southern twang said, "So y'all need to start finding some mates." The group, mostly male, suddenly became quiet while they studied the ground like there was alien life and avoided eye contact—with anyone. Mable burst out laughing, "Never mind. Let's go party y'all."

Jace kept Cassie swept up in his embrace as the mating party filtered through with their congratulations and made their way to their vehicles to head to the club. Master Bellamy hung back, intent on talking with the couple privately.

"Many felicitations, young mates." His small smile lent a melancholy air to his words.

Jace finally set Cassie down as they expressed their thanks, and Master Bellamy studied them both.

"We need you. Need you both." Master Bellamy glanced at the dispersing Guardians, the ever present concern on his face deepening. "You show us what we fight for. Those boys haven't witnessed a happy mating for... decades. Just like Kaitlyn is a breath of fresh air with her vitality and constant attitude, they—*we*—need you to keep showing us that there's more to life than the devastation Sigma can cause.

"The Sweet Mother blessed you with a mate so young, Jace. Your blessing is our blessing and we won't take her for granted again," he said, referring to how the Guardians dismissed Sigma's threat to Cassie because she was human.

"Be well." And he turned to go before either one of the pair could say anything.

Jace wrapped his arm around Cassie's slender shoulder as they watched the distinguished trainer amble off.

"Ready for the wild life, Mrs. Stockwell?" He offered to take her last name. *I'm progressive like that*, he'd told her, and started the process of becoming Jace Stockwell. It meant more as his was a general name meant to assimilate in a world he didn't belong in. It would also confuse Sigma momentarily on her status as a shifter's mate, giving Cassie time to work with him and Kaitlyn to learn more defensive maneuvers. She'd also agreed to learn how to handle and carry weapons, understanding the increased danger to her from now on, but unwilling to live a sheltered existence holed up in her new cabin at the lodge.

Cassie beamed up at him, looking radiant and more importantly—happy. "We'll do wild for the first century or two, then settle down… just a little."

Thank you for reading. I'd love to know what you thought. Please consider leaving a review at the retailor the book was purchased from.

Marie Johnston

PRIMAL CLAIM
Book Two, The Sigma Menace

After losing her family to feral shifters, Dani dedicated her life to eradicating those responsible, almost reaching Agent status with Sigma. Uncertainty about the network and questions about their "work" were plaguing her when she was tasked with a mission that would forever change her and send her running to those she once sought to destroy.

Mercury's past and unique looks kept him distant from people, even his own species. Then he captured a beautiful Sigma recruit who claimed to need his help while her scent claimed to be carrying his young.

Bitter enemies brought together, they must rely on each other to keep Sigma from getting their hands on Dani, or the growing life inside of her.

TRUE CLAIM
Book Three, The Sigma Menace

Over a century ago, Bennett Young found his mate, a human woman he trusted and was brutally betrayed by. With his one chance at happiness gone, Bennett throws himself into his work. He dreads the inevitable day he turns feral and his partners will be forced to put him down, then a routine mission brings him face-to-face with his worst nightmare. A human mate. Discovering the lovely, but evasive woman is being hunted, Bennett can't bring himself to abandon her, at least not until she's safe.

Spencer King has a boy's name and lives in the boondocks for a reason. The tall, sexy shifter who showed up on her doorstep was unwelcome…and pushy. The mating instinct she feels for him threatens everyone she's worked to keep safe. Realizing the frustrating, brooding Guardian doesn't intend to leave her alone, Spencer has to figure out if she can trust him, and to decide – stay and fight, or run for her life?

RECLAIM
Book 3.5, The Sigma Menace

Master Dane Bellamy was once the commander of the West Creek Guardians, a pack of wolf-shifters charged with protecting local shifter packs. Over a century ago, tragedy struck his growing family, driving him away with a fierce need for revenge. He returned to a devastated, withdrawn mate who resented him for leaving her to fulfill his obligations. Now, he's immersed himself in training the Guardians of his pack, while he and his mate have become nothing more than roommates, until the secret life she's been living brings danger to their doorstep. Suddenly Dane finds himself not just fighting to save his broken relationship, but their lives as well.

LAWFUL CLAIM
Book Four, The Sigma Menace

Agent E wasn't always an evil Sigma Agent. Even though evil had her claws in him, he couldn't help but hang on to his past and watch over the family he lost, protecting them by staying dead to them. Until one night, he interfered.

When Ana Esposito's life, and that of her son, was saved by the husband she had buried over a decade ago, she found her world irrevocably changed. Any chance of safety for her and her son lay with the hardened man that used to be the love of her life.

PURE CLAIM
Book Five, The Sigma Menace

Alexandria King's life was ripped away, destroyed by the evil organization Sigma, and one of its most vile leaders, Madame G. Alexandria was imprisoned, tortured, conditioned, and trained to become one of Sigma's finest Agents—Agent X. Except, despite what Sigma ordered, Agent X's only mission became keeping the secret of her bloodline and using it to destroy Madame G. She's willing to sacrifice everything to carry it out, even her own chance at happiness with her destined mate.

Guardian Commander Rhys Fitzsimmons isn't willing to let the vivacious, frustrating female, who is supposed to be his mate, throw her life away, even for such a noble cause. When her single-minded mission almost destroys her before she can carry out her destiny, he breaks all the rules to save her. But her destiny was not as they were led to believe, and the real threat to their relationship is bigger than either of them could have known.

DEMETRIUS
Book One, New Vampire Disorder

As if overthrowing the vampire government and helping implement a new council to make vampires, shifters, and hybrids play nice wasn't enough, Demetrius Devereux finds a bigger problem to deal with in an innocent, stubborn, and privileged beauty.

Callista Augustus is the over-protected daughter of a once-powerful vampire leader. Discovering her desperate father has tapped into a well of pure evil, Calli swallows her sense of betrayal and turns him in. She almost regrets it when she meets the infamous and arrogant Demetrius. Forcing herself to work with the male who ruined her family, Calli's only concern is saving her father.

When Demetrius gets past the infuriating personality of the righteous female, he realizes Calli's the one in great danger. He gives her his help out of duty, until it becomes clear that if he loses her, he loses everything.

About the Author

Marie Johnston lives in the upper Midwest with her husband, four kids, and an old cat. Recently deciding to occasionally trade in her lab coat for a laptop, she decided to write all the stories down she's been making up in her head for years. An avid reader of paranormal romance, these are the stories hanging out, waiting to be told between the demands of work, home, and the endless chauffeuring that comes with children.

mariejohnstonwriter.com
Facebook
Twitter @mjohnstonwriter

Also by Marie Johnston

The Sigma Menace:
Fever Claim (Book 1)
Primal Claim (Book 2)
True Claim (Book 3)
Reclaim (Book 3.5)
Lawful Claim (Book 4)
Pure Claim (Book 5)

New Vampire Disorder:
Demetrius (Book 1)

Fleet Week Romance:
Rebound
Shooter

Made in the USA
Coppell, TX
11 June 2020

27702669R00134